"I'm so screw

"Not necessarily," Dylan said. "Let's try to think of solutions."

Tara shook her head. "I wish I could help you, really. If I moved in here and rented out my half of the duplex, then I could pay for a better lawyer. Unfortunately, moving in with you would make me look loose, irresponsible and not much different from the wild teenager Jay's parents remember."

"Whatever you were like as a teenager shouldn't be counted against you now."

"They also could argue I don't have money, which is true, or a college education to get a higher-paying job, which is also true. Any better job I get would take away from time with Jimmy, and the salary would go toward day care and sitters instead of improving our situation."

"So the main problem is you can't provide a father," Dylan said.

"Very funny."

"I'm serious." Dylan took her hands in his. "Marry me."

Dear Reader,

Just as my deadline neared to turn in this book, my mom had a heart attack. Thankfully, she recovered enough to leave the hospital. The experience reinforced how many people grace my life with their gifts of love and friendship, and to them I'd like to say thank you.

The experience also emphasized the importance of a mother's role in her child's life. Tara Montgomery, the heroine of *The Marriage Solution*, goes to the extreme to protect her toddler—even to the point of marriage to Dylan Ross, handsome playboy with a newfound child. They help each other to survive, to heal and to love.

I enjoy hearing from my readers. Visit my website at www.megankellybooks.com, "friend" me on Facebook, or tweet me on Twitter. The Harlequin American Romance authors have a blog; my day is the seventh of each month. Visit www.harauthors.blogspot.com.

Most of all, I hope you enjoy the story of Tara and Dylan and all they go through for their children.

Best,

Megan Kelly

The Marriage Solution

MEGAN KELLY

TORONTO NEW YORK LONDON
AMSTERDAM PARIS SYDNEY HAMBURG
STOCKHOLM ATHENS TOKYO MILAN MADRID
PRAGUE WARSAW BUDAPEST AUCKLAND

Recycling programs
for this product may
not exist in your area.

ISBN-13: 978-0-373-75360-4

THE MARRIAGE SOLUTION

ABOUT THE AUTHOR

Megan Kelly grew up reading romances, never suspecting she'd one day be lucky enough to tell stories of her own. She enjoys the lighter side of life and incorporates laughter and a few tears with the family matters and romance in her books. She lives with her husband and two children in the Midwest.

Books by Megan Kelly

HARLEQUIN AMERICAN ROMANCE

Don't miss any of our special offers. Write to us at the following address for information on our newest releases.

Harlequin Reader Service
U.S.: 3010 Walden Ave., P.O. Box 1325, Buffalo, NY 14269
Canadian: P.O. Box 609, Fort Erie, Ont. L2A 5X3

This book is for mothers everywhere and
for my mom, in particular,
for all the sacrifices they make that their children
may not even know about; for my critique partners,
Carol Carson and Kimberly Killion;
and as always, for my husband. You're my rock.

Chapter One

A handsome blond stranger walked into the day care at closing, charm radiating from him like a picturesque snowbank on a bunny slope, its sparkling surface hiding a deep, dark crevasse.

Like Ted Bundy.

Tara Montgomery shuddered and stepped between the man and the doorway to the playroom where her son raced small metal cars with the one child left to be picked up. The three of them were alone with this guy, and she'd already turned out all the lights except for those in the playroom and the foyer. Rain clouds had obscured the late-May sun, leaving the room shadowed.

She swallowed down the knot warning her the man was danger. This was Howard, Missouri, after all. Population around three thousand. Crime rate around zero. Just because she'd expected to see one of the girl's parents coming to pick her up didn't mean this guy wasn't Trouble. She really had to stop watching so many TV crime shows.

"Hi." His smile widened, sharklike. "I'm guessing you're Tara."

The hairs on the back of her neck rose to alert status. He knew her name? That wasn't unusual, she assured herself, not in their small town. Maybe he had a child he wanted to enroll. Maybe he'd visited before and she was the only employee he hadn't met.

Maybe she should edge nearer to a telephone just in case she needed to call for help.

If she had to look through mug shots later, she'd remember this guy. His slate-blue eyes shone with an interest that might have been flattering if she weren't so creeped out. White teeth smiling from a tanned face generated shivers in her that were only partly fear. Six feet tall or so with long legs in twill slacks, broad shoulders filling out a butter-yellow polo shirt, and large, well-kept hands. The perfect size for caressing a woman…or strangling her.

Get real. Small town, small dangers. The pep talk restored her usual confidence. "Yes, I'm Tara. How can I help you?"

He extended his hand. "I'm Dylan Ross. Is my mom in her office?"

"Oh, gosh, I'm sorry." Tara wiped her sweaty hand on her work apron, feeling the heat in her face even as her body sagged with relief. The boss's son—and she'd been memorizing his face for a police lineup. Jeez. She shook his hand, noticing the strength he held in check. His gentleness warmed her to him. She knew his reputation as Mr. Love 'Em and Leave 'Em, but her body didn't listen to her brain. Too many women had declared him Mr. Love 'Em and Leave 'Em Smiling.

His sun-bleached hair and tan had probably been gained on one of his trips scuba diving in the Caribbean that Betty—her boss and his mom—had told Tara about. He took his widowed mother out to dinner every other week and helped his brother and sister-in-law with their eight children. Strong, handsome, family-oriented. She sighed, a little wistful.

Don't even think about it, the little voice in her head warned. Even his mother described him as a "ladies' man." Tara had had one go-round with an undependable good-time guy like that, and had learned her lesson.

"I should have recognized you from the pictures in your mom's office," she said. "You're the computer son."

He quirked one eyebrow in question.

"Process of elimination, since I've met your brother a few times when he's picked up the twins and Caitlyn. Adam builds houses, right?"

"Right." He grinned. "Although being called 'the computer son' makes me sound like a robot."

"Your mom's at a meeting. The town Founder's Day planning, I think. She said she might be late."

"We're going to dinner. I'm surprised she didn't call me."

"But it's Wednesday." Tara cringed at her exclamation. Betty and Dylan had a set dinner date every other Tuesday. Tara left at three o'clock on Tuesdays and Thursdays, which was why she hadn't met him before tonight. She wished she hadn't made it so obvious how much she knew about the man's life.

Dylan cocked his head. "I was out of town yesterday."

"Sorry." She stuck her hands in her jeans pockets, feeling like a stalker herself. A quick glance at Jimmy and Hannah, now encircling themselves with multicolored blocks, eliminated the possibility of using them as an excuse to escape. "I feel like I know you. Your mom talks about you and Adam all the time."

He winced comically. "I can only imagine."

"You come off pretty good, usually." Depending on one's outlook, that could be true. Betty's stories of his escapades were related with parental amusement. Tara didn't find the ones of him as an adult, dating every woman he saw, all that humorous. But his preteen years sounded endearing, just as she imagined Jimmy would be one day too soon—curious and adventurous, collecting bugs and rocks and playing sports to drain off his boundless energy.

"Usually?" Dylan chuckled. "I guess I should be grateful for even that concession. Adam and I didn't give her and Dad an easy time when we were growing up."

A smile tugged the corner of her mouth against her will. "So I've heard. She calls you 'the boy terror.'"

Their gazes caught. The admiration in his eyes reminded her of when she was just a woman, not a mom. Back when she could have flirted a little and encouraged him to ask her out. When she would have been free to accept a dinner invitation…or more. Ah, the good old days.

Four long years ago. Before the mistake that had become the greatest blessing of her life—getting pregnant with Jimmy. Now she wanted stability and a future, not just a good time.

"Mom's told me a little about you and your son, too." He glanced over her shoulder at the kids in the playroom before returning to meet her gaze.

She searched his expression, pleased to find no reproach. She wasn't up to a debate on single parenthood.

"Mom says you've been a godsend here."

Tara hunched her shoulders, embarrassed. Betty had overstated the matter. "Oh, I don't know about that."

"I do." He stepped nearer and, despite her better intentions, her skin prickled with awareness. "I want to thank you for how you've eased the burden for Mom. The office work pretty much overwhelmed her. She'd never have been able to take this trip to Europe without you to run the office while she's gone."

"She should have had help long before this. The woman juggles like magic." Tara realized they stood only a foot apart now. She felt his pull like the moon's on the tide.

"She has, up till lately, but her age is catching up to her."

Tara waved a hand in dismissal, almost hitting him in the chest. His hard, broad chest. She swallowed, fighting the urge to test its firmness with her hand. "If she's slowed down any, I wouldn't know it. She has more energy than I do."

"Maybe, but I still wish she wouldn't go. I'd be happier if she stayed here where I know she's safe."

This near to him, she could feel the heat of his body. He smelled like sunshine and the threat of rain and...a man. A scent she hadn't had a chance to enjoy in quite some time.

Self-conscious now, she tucked a strand of her shoulder-length hair behind her ear. Get back to the subject.

Wait. Had he really said he wanted his mom to stay home from her dream trip to Europe just so he wouldn't have to worry about her? She must have misunderstood. She took a step backward to gain distance and perspective. "Is there something wrong with Betty's health to prevent her from traveling?"

"Not particularly. But she's sixty-seven. You never know what could happen."

Tara frowned. "She's going to be with tour groups and traveling with friends in between the tours."

"For three months? It bothers me. She's never been one to travel."

His smile edged over into being a tad too patronizing to ignore. Tara put her hands on her hips, willing herself to hear him out. "Then maybe it's about time she did."

"I think you've misunderstood me." He stepped forward, closing in, filling her lungs with his scent, making her eyes go wide at the surprising electricity. "Maybe we could discuss it over dinner?"

The chirping of his cell phone cut off her response. Which was fortunate, as she didn't know what she'd say.

Yes? Tara determined to clear her head as he mouthed "sorry" and stepped away to take the call.

"Marissa." His deep voice caressed the woman's name. "Of course. I was going to call you this evening."

Tara's jaw set as he walked farther away, presumably for privacy. She didn't want to hear him sweet-talk some woman. The reminder of his playboy lifestyle settled the decision. Dinner with him? Not likely.

Dylan returned with a cat-ate-the-canary smile. "Sorry for the interruption. Now, what were we talking about?"

"When your mom will be back. I expected her before this."

His eyebrows drew together as he did a quick study of her expression. Then he nodded his concession. Smart man, recognizing a lost cause.

"I'll call her cell phone," he said. "See if the meeting's over yet."

His phone rang again. "Maybe that's her now."

He flicked a glance at the display. "Hmm. I don't recognize the number. That's out of state."

A long-distance booty call? Tara showed her teeth in a smile he couldn't misinterpret as friendly.

After a second's deliberation, he pocketed the phone, letting the call go to voice mail, and stepped backward. "I guess I'll be leaving then. Are you going to be okay here alone?"

"Yes, but thanks for asking." His thoughtfulness shouldn't affect her. "I won't be too far behind you."

A clatter cut off further words. Jimmy chortled, eyeing the spilled blocks. Hannah beamed with an equal amount of pride.

Tara gave Dylan a wry glance. "Or maybe I'll be a few minutes longer than I'd planned." She walked toward the kids. "You know what happens when you make a mess."

"Kean up, kean up," they sang.

"Nice to meet you," Tara said to Dylan. She knelt beside the children and joined them in the cleanup song. They should pick up the blocks themselves, but helping gave her an excuse to evade Dylan. Glancing over her shoulder, she noted he stood watching.

He backed away, keeping his eyes on hers. "It was nice to meet you, too, Tara. Very nice."

Despite knowing he was a womanizer, she couldn't deny the pleasure his words produced. Darn it. Seemed she had a type, after all. Good thing she'd grown out of it, though.

She reminded herself of that all evening.

By the next morning, she had to drag herself and poor Jimmy to the day care to open at five-thirty. Not a chance she'd admit Dylan Ross had kept her awake most of the night. Sure, images of his smile, and memories of his intriguing scent, his deep voice and the humor in his eyes had made her toss and turn. But that was irritation. Irritated that he was wasting his time, his looks, and his perfectly good genes on one-night stands. Irritated that he'd received a phone call from another woman just as he'd asked her out. Irritated that she hadn't had the chance to shut down his game and prove that some women were immune to his so-called charms.

Because she would have said no. She was almost positive.

It was the "almost" which had kept her awake. Not Dylan Ross but her own uncertainty.

Tara stifled a yawn as she approached the day care, juggling her work keys in one hand and keeping hold of her squirming son's hand with her other. Neither of them had wanted to roll out of their beds when the morning sun had yet to perk up the gloomy gray sky.

"Are you Tara Montgomery?" a male voice asked from behind her.

She squealed and pivoted toward the man, who had stepped out of nowhere. Instinctively, she pushed three-year-old Jimmy against the building and blocked him with her body.

The man stood waiting, a half smile—a darned scary half smile—on his face. He was bland and forgettable, other than starting to go bald and being slightly paunchy. No child accompanied him, so why was he hanging around a day care at 5:30 a.m.? For the first time, she wished she didn't open by herself three days a week. Betty would be lethal swinging a broom.

Tara scanned the parking area, but no one else had arrived, nor did she expect anyone for fifteen long minutes.

Fight or flight? She wasn't much of a fighter, unless the almost too-normal guy threatened her son. As for flight, she wouldn't get far, as she'd have to carry Jimmy.

Whoa, she admonished herself. She'd thought these things last night, and the stranger had turned out to be the boss's son. This guy was probably some long-lost cousin.

Calling on years of bravado she'd used facing her overbearing parents, she took a deep breath. Arching an eyebrow to look imperious and heaving a sigh to appear too-busy-to-be-bothered, Tara faced down the stranger. "Yes?"

"So you are Tara Montgomery? Tara Scarlett Montgomery?"

A wince broke her facade. "That's me, unfortunately."

How did he know—?

"I have a delivery for you."

"Oh!" She grinned as relief swept through her, leaving her feeling foolish for suspecting another innocuous man of being a maniac killer.

He handed her a brown envelope. "You've been served."

Dread squeezed her heart as he walked away. *Innocuous, my ass.*

"Mommy? Who was that?"

Tara sifted through her vocabulary for a description appropriate for her son to hear. Then her sense of fairness kicked in; he was only doing his job. "Just a delivery man, like Cedric, our mailman."

"Oh." Jimmy fidgeted, and she realized she still held him pressed against the building.

She stepped away. "Sorry, baby."

"I'm not a baby."

"Right. Sorry again, puddin' pie."

He giggled, and her day settled back on its axis.

After she settled Jimmy to one of the morning chores to keep him occupied, Tara ripped open the envelope. She scanned the letter, then read it once again, frozen with anxiety.

Jimmy's paternal grandparents were suing her for custody.

She fell into a chair, stunned.

The grounds for the hearing cited her being unfit to raise a child. She unclenched her teeth and conceded they would have had a point if she were the girl they remembered. As a teenager, she'd partied, drank, stayed out late, and had numerous boyfriends before their son, Jay. She'd been a typical rich girl with too much money, too much free time, and too few responsibilities.

Then the stick had turned blue.

Not only had her life changed with her pregnancy, but she'd changed her life. However, since the first of those life-changing steps had been to leave home, his parents couldn't know she'd become a responsible adult and a good mother.

Her own parents hadn't wanted her to have the baby. Tara had fled and, aside from monthly phone calls home to assure them she was fine, had stayed missing for the past four years. She'd left it to Jay to tell his family. Admittedly, she'd been a coward, not wanting to face their censure after her own parents' rejection.

She didn't know what motivated the Summerfields, but the obvious solution made her shudder. Visiting her parents to uncover what they knew about their friends' plans was out of the question, not after the things they'd said to her. She'd had four years to remake herself, and she liked the person she'd become.

Her stomach clenched. *Could* the courts take away Jimmy based on her past? How would she prove she'd changed? That she, an unwed day-care assistant who struggled to make ends meet, provided the best home for her son? Or would the judge look at Jay's ultrawealthy parents, with their stable life in a two-adult household, and decide in their favor?

She didn't know any lawyers and probably couldn't afford a good one. She regretted not collecting her trust fund two years before on her twenty-first birthday. Her parents had probably closed access to it when she'd refused to have an abortion. She knew how their minds worked. On the off chance they hadn't remembered, she'd call their bank and check.

Would they take her side now, or would they see this hearing as an unexpected gift—someone responsible to take over the care of Jimmy for her? To "free" her of her "mistake" and let her go back to her old lifestyle. As though she'd ever want that life again. She only wanted Jimmy.

For the rest of the day, she tried to stuff the worry to the back of her mind. She painted pictures, served snacks, and kept her monsters at bay by concentrating on the children. Too upset to eat, she spent her lunch break poring over lawyers' information in the phone book and on the internet. They were all just names to her. She made notes of the families at the day care who'd endured custody battles, intending to call the people she knew for recommendations. And the people she didn't personally know. And the people she'd only heard of through someone else. Embarrassing herself didn't matter. Nothing mattered except keeping Jimmy.

Tara looked over at him at the snack table, talking to his classmates and wearing a purple grape juice mustache, his shirt covered with crumbs. Tonight she'd snuggle him and read his favorite books and watch his favorite movie.

She'd worry about getting a lawyer tomorrow. She smirked and raised her grape juice cup in a toast to her namesake. After all, tomorrow *was* another day.

DYLAN UNLOCKED THE DOOR to his condo, irritated and tired after the dinner with his mom that they'd put off from the night before. Their biweekly date was as much about spending time with her as it was about checking up on her health and well-being. Tonight, however, she'd done nothing but talk about what a "godsend" Tara Montgomery was. He didn't know why his mom's assistant had taken an instant dislike to him. He also didn't know why it bothered him that she had.

Tara would take over while his mom spent three months in Europe. He didn't like the idea of his mother being on her own that long. A sixty-seven-year-old woman needed to stay home and take care of her business, even if she was in decent health. What would Adam do without their mom to help with his kids?

What would Dylan do with her so far away? His attending university then working on the West Coast had been different. Somehow.

Every time he'd tried to change the subject at dinner, his mom steered the conversation back to Tara. He pictured her as he'd seen her, annoyed with him, not backing down to her employer's son, not treating him with respect. And, okay, he'd admit it, not accepting his invitation to dinner.

His mom constantly bringing up her name meant he couldn't stop thinking about her. Her long black lashes set off blue eyes that enticed him like a deep lake. He'd like to dive in and see what mysteries they concealed. The white-gold of her shoulder-length hair tempted his fingers to test its silkiness. If she hadn't turned into such a shrew, he might have made a more serious play for her.

Flipping through a mental file of available women, he considered who he'd call for a date the next night, not planning to spend another evening alone with his thoughts. Tara Montgomery flashed into his mind, making him scowl. She was *so* not what he needed. He wanted someone to flirt with, to laugh with, and by evening's end, probably make love with. That last thought—and the images of Tara it produced—had him trying to clear his mind. She was entirely wrong for him. Too serious.

One date with her and she'd be hearing wedding bells. His brother would ride him about starting a family, and how Dylan should catch up to him in the baby-making department.

Eight kids. Dylan shook his head. He might love being an uncle, but he was in no way ready to start a family.

He searched for his cell phone, thinking of Marissa's offer the night before, knowing he'd call her. She was fun, easy to be with and didn't expect any promises from him. Her dark hair and brown eyes were as different from Tara's as he could need.

Before he could pick up the phone, it rang. Anticipation had him smiling. Fate had made the decision for him—as long as the caller was a woman other than his mother, he'd found the next evening's distraction.

"This is Violet Durant," the voice on the phone informed Dylan after his eager hello. "Rosemary Durant's mother."

For a moment, his mind remained a blank, then he remembered Rose, a woman he'd dated for about eight months in California. A vivacious redhead, as he recalled, always in good spirits. He hadn't heard from her in years. He wouldn't mind seeing Rose again, but why would her mother call him? "What can I do for you?"

"I'm sorry to call so late, but I hadn't heard from you about when you're arriving, even though I've called several times. You are going to make it here in time for the funeral, aren't you?"

The news hit him like a physical blow. Bubbly Rose Durant dead? "I'm so sorry. I didn't know she'd passed. I didn't even know she was ill." *Idiot. Stop babbling.* Rose could have been in a car wreck. "Or was it…?"

"A brain tumor."

"I'm sorry, Mrs. Durant."

"But you are going to come to the funeral, aren't you?"

"Of course." What else could he say? He hadn't seen Rose in—what, five years?—and God help him, he hadn't thought about her in nearly that long either. But he'd hardly admit that to her grieving mother.

"Good. I figured you would, although it would have been nice to hear it confirmed before this. I need to know what your plans are for Lily."

Dylan frowned at her tone and her assumption that he'd known about Rosemary. Then her last statement diverted him. What plans? What *Lily?* He groaned. It would have appealed to Rose's sense of humor to leave him one of her mange-infected dogs.

Mrs. Durant inhaled deeply. "I can't take her home to Boston with me, due to my health. As much as it pains me to say it, I'm just not capable of caring for her."

He could hardly believe his bad luck. Rosemary had been crazy about animals. She'd taken in five stray, worm-infested dogs and one bedraggled, pregnant alley cat in the eight months he'd known her. He shuddered. At least he hadn't lived with her. If her mother wanted him to adopt some stray, he couldn't turn her down, not while she grieved the loss of her daughter. She must be unable to exercise the dog or perhaps she had cat allergies.

"I'll make sure Lily has a good home." He reviewed the women he knew again. Surely one was a sucker for stray animals? Or, he thought with a grin, maybe it was time for Adam's kids to get a pet. "It's the least I can do."

Silence hung in the airwaves until Dylan had to double-check the connection. The woman couldn't read his mind, could she? Guilt had him second-guessing himself. He could care for a pet. He could put food and water in bowls and take it out twice a day to do its business. It would be even better if Lily turned out to be a cat, as they were more independent.

Maybe it wouldn't hurt to have someone to come home to. Surely when he had to travel, someone would take care of the thing.

"Do you have anyone to watch the poor darling when you're gone?" Violet asked.

He stared at the phone. Maybe she *could* read his mind. That scary voodoo mothers had. But he wasn't about to get gooey over an animal and treat it like a human. Violet would naturally be emotional, this being her last tie with Rosemary. Would she expect Christmas cards signed with little paw prints?

"Leaving home and living with you will be a traumatic change," Violet continued, "especially after enduring Rosemary's death. Maybe you have someplace in mind she could go during the day when you're at work?"

Dylan snorted. Like he could afford that. Still, he used a reasonable tone when he countered, "I'm sorry. We'll have to talk more about this when I get there, but I just can't see providing day care for an animal."

Violet gasped. "Lily's not an animal. She's your daughter."

Chapter Two

"I'm going to have to take some time off," Dylan told his business partner, Joe Riley, on the phone fifteen minutes later. He jammed some socks into his overnight bag, then turned to reach for underwear. He didn't have time for this call. Should have made it from the car. Still, he'd found himself reaching for his cell phone. Of anyone Dylan could have talked to, Joe would understand. He'd married a woman with two kids, becoming an instant father, and he'd also known Rosemary when Dylan and Joe had worked together in California, so explanations wouldn't take as long. Dylan dreaded the calls he'd have to make to his mother and brother.

"What's going on?" Concern layered Joe's words. "You never take unscheduled time off. Is it your mom?"

"No, it's my daughter."

"Your *what?*"

"Yeah, that was pretty much my reaction, too." He reached for his black suit, then realized he'd need his garment bag, not his duffel. Formal occasions, funerals. "I'm trying to pack now. Got to get going soon. Hold on, I'm putting you on speaker."

"The hell you are. I'll be right over."

"I don't have time—" Dylan realized Joe had hung up.

He set down his phone and retrieved his garment bag from the back of the closet.

Twelve minutes later, he opened the door of his condo to Joe. Dylan had finished packing—or in this case, throwing clothes into luggage—with little thought and less care. He needed to get on the road.

He needed to get to his daughter.

"I ran every red light to get here," Joe said. "Now, say that again."

Dylan smirked and turned toward his bedroom to get his bag. "I have a daughter. Lily. She's four years old."

"Who's the mother?"

Dylan detoured to the kitchen. He'd called Joe for a reason, and it wasn't just to report about work. Reaching into the fridge, he grabbed two Cokes and handed one to his friend. The occasion called for beer, both to mourn Rose and to celebrate his "new" daughter—hell, he should pass around cigars—but he was about to drive three hours into the middle of nowhere and needed a clear head. "Rosemary Durant. Do you remember her?"

"No."

"Redhead, curvaceous, big laugh."

"No."

"Really fun—or so I thought at the time. Kind of wild and irreverent."

Joe's eyes widened. "The one from San Francisco?"

"You're slow tonight. If I fathered a kid who's four now, it would have been when you and I worked for Amerfacton in California."

"*If* you fathered a kid?"

Dylan shook his head. "I didn't mean it like that. I'm sure. Rose wouldn't have told her mom it was me unless I'm Lily's father."

"Why did Rose contact you now, after all this time? Does she want child support?"

"I wish." He took a drink of his pop to still the churning in his gut. "Rosemary passed away from a brain tumor. Her mother called to see what I planned to do about Lily."

Joe's face expressed his sorrow. "Oh, man, Dyl. I'm sorry."

"Yeah, me, too." Dylan paused. "I think Mrs. Durant wants to find out if she can trust me with Lily before she goes back to Boston. She doesn't think much of me, neglecting my daughter all this time."

"But it's not your fault. You didn't know."

Dylan clapped his hand on his friend's shoulder, touched that Joe hadn't had to ask. He knew Dylan would have done the right thing if Rose had told him. "That surprised her. She thought I'd abandoned them both."

Joe studied him over the top of the can while Dylan drank. "What are you going to do, bring her back here? Or does Rose's mom want her?"

"She says she can't care for her, but I'll check that out. I mean, I would send money for her care. Isn't that the best thing, for her to be raised by a woman?"

"Have you thought about this at all? What you're giving up?"

"Look, I know you just became Father of the Year, but it's not for everyone. What do I know about kids?"

Joe's laugh held little humor. "I'm sure in the past ten years, you've picked up a thing or two from Adam's kids."

"I'm their uncle. I come in, we play, I leave. A dad is full-time."

"It sure is. Having Abby and Bobby in my life has enriched it more than I could imagine. I hope Lisa and I have a couple more."

Dylan shook his head. "Not the same thing, Joe. I don't have a wife to help with Lily. My spare bedroom is full of junk; the other bedroom is an office. I don't even have a bed for Lily. What about her things? Where would I put them?"

Joe shook his head. "Details. But just you thinking about all this proves you know what you're doing. More than I did when I started seeing Lisa. I screwed up with her kids plenty before getting the hang of it."

"I don't know anything about raising a child, especially a girl."

"She's your daughter. And nobody really knows what they're doing at the beginning. You have your family. They'll be a great support, after the shock wears off."

Dylan set his pop on the counter with deliberate care. He shifted, bracing his feet apart. "The kid doesn't know me. It's not like starting out with a baby. Maybe she'd be better off with her grandma. With a woman."

"Weren't you planning to have kids someday?"

"My plans obviously don't count for crap. Rose raised Lily without telling me. Now, after the other choices don't work out, I get a call out of the blue. 'Come get your daughter.'"

"Dyl, don't go to the funeral pissed off."

"I don't have much choice." He blew out a breath. "But I hear you. I'll keep it under control."

Joe shook his head, as though realizing Dylan's mind wouldn't be changed. "When's your flight? I'll drive you to the airport."

"I'm not flying. She and Lily have been living in Salina."

"Kansas?" When Dylan nodded, he continued, "What was she doing in Kansas?"

Dylan eyed him, feeling grim. "I'll let you know when I find out."

TARA PACED around the coffee table in her living room the next night, watching her cell phone as though it were an anaconda about to swallow her whole. The bank had confirmed her fears—her parents had blocked access to her trust through some legal maneuver. A good attorney could probably circumvent whatever they'd done since she was now of legal age, but she had neither the time nor the money to go that route.

When she'd jokingly wailed, "Where's all my money?" the clerk asked her to hold. Before she could explain her lame sense of humor, he informed her the Certificate of Deposit from Virginia Harris had come to term if she wished to cash it in.

Oh, brother, did she!

Bless Grandmother Harris. She'd spread her considerable fortune among her five grandchildren. Trusts, Certificates of Deposit, stocks—the crafty old magpie had safeguarded the funds from Tara's dad and uncles. On her nineteenth birthday, Tara had withdrawn every dollar she could liquidate to prepay her doctor and hospital bills and buy the duplex she still lived in. She thought she'd used everything her grandmother had left her, but it seemed Granny had undisclosed secrets.

The sum wouldn't secure an attorney of the same caliber as the firm Jay's parents retained, but Tara could at least approach a reputable lawyer now.

Still, the phone lay in view, taunting her. Would a telephone call fix anything? Perhaps her parents would know what had motivated Jay's parents to act now. Could she resolve her problems by talking to her parents and having them contact the Summerfields? Or would dealing with them now make matters worse?

But what would be worse than losing Jimmy? They couldn't possibly threaten her with anything more frightening.

She took a deep breath, picked up the phone and punched in her parents' phone number. With any luck, they'd be out golfing in the moonlight and she could leave a message with a maid. At least she could tell herself she'd tried.

Coward. She swallowed the moisture pooling in her mouth as the phone on the other end rang. Then she heard her mother's greeting. Closing her eyes, Tara suppressed her longing for home. She wasn't six anymore. She no longer believed in the Easter Bunny or the tooth fairy or the fantasy of parents more concerned with their daughter than themselves.

"Hi, Mom."

"Tara?" Her mother's strident voice came sharply through the earpiece.

"Yeah. I mean, yes," she corrected, remembering her mother's preference for the proper use of the English language. "How are you?"

The derision in her mother's chuckle chafed Tara's ear.

"You don't care how we are," Janine Montgomery said. "You wouldn't have called at all if you hadn't received notice of the hearing."

Tara closed her eyes again, glad she'd asked Kim, the teenage girl next door, to watch Jimmy. He wouldn't have to witness her reaction to this call. "I did receive the papers, yes. So you know what the Summerfields are doing to me?"

"We heard at the club, and in the most humiliating way. They haven't spoken to us directly. It's been four lost years for them. The same four years we've spent worrying about you."

"I've called you. Every month." She'd maintained the same cell phone number in case they wanted to reach her, but had kept her location a secret.

She'd been in the background of a photograph featured in a recent newspaper article on the Wee Care. Small and grainy, the shot hadn't looked anything like her and she'd shrugged off her apprehension. Now it seemed she'd have been better off avoiding cameras.

"Those weren't phone calls," her mom insisted. "Those were news briefs. You never said more than 'we're doing okay.'"

Tara slumped onto the couch. Was that pain in her mother's voice? "I'm sorry. I didn't want you to worry, but I couldn't come back."

"You didn't have to leave in the first place."

"You and Dad didn't want me to have Jimmy. I couldn't stay."

"You embarrassed us in front of our friends. What were we supposed to tell them when they asked about you?"

Tara straightened. Her daughter left home, pregnant and alone, and all her mother cared about was the gossip it caused? "Your *friends?*"

"We haven't been able to socialize with the Summerfields since."

"You're worried about *Jay's* family?" Tara thought her mom and dad would be angry with Jay for running out on her, and by extension, not be on speaking terms with his parents. Them suing her for custody should have put an end to any tenuous relationship they'd had.

"Well, it wasn't their fault you got pregnant."

Tara's jaw dropped. Followed by the phone as she disconnected.

Calling had definitely made things worse. It had not only wounded her, but had destroyed her last hope someone could talk some sense into Jay's parents.

DYLAN SQUEEZED the bridge of his nose, blocking off the headache caused by tension and his new daughter's unceasing weeping. Every time he saw her, Lily had her back to a wall, her eyes fixed on him, and tears pouring down her face, accompanied by sobs, which became louder if he approached. Rosemary's mother sometimes rocked her, bathed her face with a cold rag, or otherwise tried to console his child, but nothing worked for long.

In her late fifties, Violet Durant had a solid, no-nonsense quality about her. She'd probably be good at raising a little girl alone—better than Dylan was coping, anyway. The last several days of stress getting to know his grieving daughter and the nights when he'd lain awake with bitter thoughts about her mother had left his brain fried. But Violet also walked with a cane due to her arthritis. He'd seen her at the end of the day, barely able to move, and knew her taking in Lily wasn't an option.

Dylan's jaw ached to the point where he could barely unclench his teeth. Fortunately, everyone had gone away, leaving him, Violet and Lily in the echoing silence of Rosemary's house. Not one of Rose's friends had been surprised to learn he was Lily's father. Apparently, she'd told everyone except him. She'd lived less than three hours away, with his child, and had never contacted him. None of the people he'd asked could—or would—tell him why Rose had moved to Salina from California, especially when her mom lived in Massachusetts. Since Violet had no idea, either, he doubted he'd ever get the answer.

She reached across the sofa cushion and put a hand on his arm. "I want to apologize again for Rosemary. She should have told you when she discovered she was pregnant, no matter what happened to your relationship. It's not right you didn't know about Lily."

"Even seeing Lily, it's hard to believe she's real, that she's mine." He glanced across the room, where his four-year-old daughter—his *daughter*—rocked a doll in her arms. At least Lily had stopped sobbing for the moment, which she'd been doing since his arrival two days before. Now she just looked lost and alone, which wasn't any easier to bear.

Glancing back, he caught the affront on Violet's face. "Oh, no, I didn't mean that the way it sounded. I know Lily is mine." He'd have to watch his phrasing—first Joe, now his child's grandmother. "It's just a jolt to see her, not only the fact of her existence, but that's she already four. I missed so much, and she's so…"

His chest ached, but he didn't have a word to describe his daughter. Yes, she was beautiful, but looks wouldn't have mattered. Yes, she was haunting in her grief, and breaking his heart, but he would have felt this way even if she were sunny and affectionate. This feeling was something else, something deeper. Something that made his chest hurt.

Violet had tamed Lily's wavy, waist-length cinnamon hair into a ponytail. Unfortunately, the style exposed her pale, freckled face and red-rimmed eyes. However much he'd fallen in love with her from the first moment, Lily avoided him like the stranger he was.

"For the record," he said, "Rose and I didn't break up. We just stopped seeing each other. I don't remember any one thing in particular, no fight or anything. Did she ever mention anything to you?" *Like why she didn't tell me about our baby? Why she moved to Kansas?*

Violet shook her head. "I'm sorry, no. She stopped talking about you, until she told me about the pregnancy, that is. I just assumed you didn't want either of them."

"I would have." He looked into the bright green eyes his daughter had inherited. Despite his panic and dread, he felt sure he'd have done the right thing. "I would have married Rose and been a father to Lily."

"I'm sorry for all the rotten things I thought about you." She smiled weakly.

"You're welcome to visit us any time you can get away from your florist shop."

Violet nodded. "I will. I'll be flying to Kansas City so often you'll wish you'd never said that. But you can't take it back now."

"Lily will need both her grandmas. You'll always be family."

Violet Durant, the woman who would have been his mother-in-law, collapsed in his arms, her shoulders shaking with silent tears.

THE WEEKEND CRAWLED BY despite the Memorial Day celebrations, as did the following Tuesday and Wednesday. Tara researched attorneys on the internet, reading through websites and newspaper articles when she could find them. Few lawyers listed their success rate in family cases, and she wouldn't have trusted those who did. A few day-care parents had gone to family court, but most cases involving custody of children also involved divorce. One couple had adopted a child who attended the Wee Care. Tara called everyone she could think of, no matter how well or how little she knew them. She got some referrals to further her research, but she had to make a decision on a lawyer soon.

Tara returned from her afternoon stint in the day-care room on Wednesday to hear Betty talking in her office. The door stood ajar. A deeper, masculine voice spoke. Thinking Betty might need her to take a child to the playroom so she could talk privately to prospective parents, Tara poked her head around the door.

Dylan sat in a chair across from his mother's desk. His stubbled chin and tired eyes shouldn't have touched Tara's heart, but Betty had told her of his recent discovery. Tara couldn't help but compare him to her ex-boyfriend, Jay, who also had a love-'em-and-leave-'em attitude. As evidenced by his sudden trip to Portugal when she'd told him they'd conceived. She pulled back from the doorway, hoping Betty hadn't—

"Tara," her boss called. "Come in and meet Lily, my granddaughter."

Tara set her shoulders and plastered a smile on her face. Once inside, she avoided meeting Dylan's gaze, her eyes all for the waif standing against the far wall.

"Hello, Lily." She spoke softly in case the girl was easily spooked. Her defensive position spoke volumes about her unease.

Large green eyes lifted to her face, and Tara's heart melted. "I'm Miss Tara."

Lily glided across the room. "Hi."

The child whispered the word, then grabbed on to the folds of Tara's pant leg. Their gazes locked for a moment before Lily laid her cheek against Tara's thigh.

Betty's slightly open mouth communicated her astonishment. Tara didn't understand the situation, but the tension in the room enveloped her like sticky cobwebs.

Dylan's jaw flexed, his eyes unreadable. "I guess that settles it. Looks like Lily's found a soul mate. She should be happy here."

Tara frowned at him. Why was he so surly? Didn't he want his daughter to be comfortable coming to the Wee Care? A check of her boss's desktop gave her an idea for escape. "Betty, do you need the forms for Lily's registration? I can get the papers from the file cabinet."

Betty nodded, and Tara eased Lily away. When she turned to leave, the little girl followed so closely she stepped on Tara's heel. Dylan's gaze burned into Tara while she retrieved the correct documents. She walked back to her employer's office as reluctantly as Lily did, but resisted the urge to drag her feet like the child.

"Is there anything else you need?" she asked Betty.

"Please sit down, Tara. I don't want to impose, but Lily seems to have taken a shine to you."

"What my mother means," Dylan said in a hard tone, "is that you're the *only* one she's 'taken a shine to.' Including me."

Tara slid into a chair, the child at her side. Poor thing. No wonder the girl hadn't warmed up to him if he used that gritty manner all the time. Didn't he know how sensitive children were to nuances? If Tara could hear the resentment in his voice, so would Lily.

And why should he be resentful? Because he had to raise his daughter since her mother had *died?* She clenched her teeth, holding back the words that would not only get her fired, but hurt both Betty and Lily. She couldn't remember what she'd ever found attractive about him.

Liar.

Tara flinched from the voice of her conscience and glanced down at Lily. Tears streaked the girl's face. When had she started crying? Tara pulled her up onto her lap. The restraint with which Lily cried, as though the situation were hopeless, tore at her heart. To a little girl who'd recently lost her mother, it probably felt true. Tara cuddled her and kissed the top of her head.

Lily started quietly sobbing, the small noise all the more upsetting as she broke her previous silence. Tara darted a look at Betty and Dylan. Betty half rose from her chair, but Dylan waved her back down.

"She cries a lot," he said, in a resigned tone. "I can take her."

"I'm fine." Tara rocked the girl against her. "This is hardly my first experience with a crying child."

"We'll take good care of Lily here," Betty assured him. "She'll adjust, Dylan. It's only going to take time."

"Do you think it will be a problem?" he asked, looking at Tara. "Mom said no, but I have a feeling you'll be honest. Will it upset the other children if Lily doesn't stop crying?"

"Dylan," Betty said, "of course she'll stop. This is all so upsetting for her. A new home, a new parent, the person she depended on not being in the picture any longer."

Even though Betty delicately phrased the passing of Lily's mom, Tara frowned as they discussed Lily as though the girl couldn't hear.

He ran a hand down his face. "I might be able to take some time off, maybe work from home for a couple of weeks."

"She'll settle down," Betty insisted.

"I hope so, Mom. But if she takes a while, Tara?"

She felt the girl shudder against her. She rubbed a hand over Lily's back and impulsively hugged her closer. "Lily will be fine with us."

Tara would make darn sure of it. Whatever it took, she'd guarantee this poor, grief-ridden girl had a safe place to land.

Chapter Three

Engrossed in her finances later that night, Tara jumped when the phone rang. She darted a glance at the clock as she rushed to answer before the ringing woke Jimmy. Ten-thirty. Who would be calling at this hour? Naturally, her mind leapt to disasters. Hospitals and ambulances, car accidents and heart attacks. But she couldn't imagine who would have her listed as an emergency contact.

"Tara? This is Dylan Ross."

Fear dried out her mouth. *Betty.* "Yes?"

"I hate to impose, but I need a favor. And I know we don't really know one another well enough for me to ask, but…"

She could hear Lily crying in the background. Were they at the hospital? "What is it, Dylan?"

"Could you come over to my place? I can't get Lily to settle down. She's nearly hysterical."

To his place? Was this a line? But Lily's distress and the tension in Dylan's tone painted a more logical picture.

"It's Lily? Not your mom?"

His exhalation sounded in her ear. "No. Sorry to alarm you. Mom's fine as far as I know. The problem is Lily. I can't get her to sleep."

The knot in her stomach loosened. Tara glanced down

the short hall leading to the bedrooms. She'd have to awaken her child to comfort his. While it pained her to think of Lily crying inconsolably, she resented Dylan turning to her for a convenient solution. He should learn to take care of Lily himself and not rely on a near stranger.

"I wouldn't ask, but I'm afraid she'll make herself sick. Since she bonded with you today at the day care, I thought—I hoped—you'd be able to calm her down."

"Jimmy's asleep."

"Oh."

He didn't add anything. Tara waited a moment for him to come up with an alternative.

"I'd send you one of Adam's babysitters," he said, "but they're mostly high school kids, and they have school tomorrow. His daytime sitter might be available, but she has three kids in elementary school who she couldn't leave alone."

Tara sighed inwardly as he thought aloud. None of his options would work well. He must have tried everything on his own if he'd searched for this many solutions already. "I'll come."

"What about your son?"

"I'll have to bring him."

"I'm really sorry, Tara. If there was another way, I wouldn't ask."

She made a noncommittal sound, which he could interpret however he chose. Comforting a child wasn't rocket science. Yet she'd noticed how Lily had kept her distance from him. His daughter may not be able to accept comfort from him so soon after meeting him. He'd disrupted her life, arrived when her mom was being buried, and taken Lily away from her home. Tara could understand her confusion and resentment, as well as his desperation.

"I owe you big-time."

"Let's see if I can do anything for her first."

"It's enough that you're coming and that you have to wake your son. I'm sorry to have to ask you to do this."

Did he mean sorry to ask, or sorry to ask *her,* she wondered as she wrote down his directions.

She wrapped Jimmy in a light blanket but tried not to rouse him. Perhaps he'd get through the coming hour or so without fully waking. Yeah, she thought. And then she'd win the big Lotto jackpot.

The drive took just ten minutes. Only a few other cars passed her, with drivers heading to their nice soft beds. Lamplight flooded the parking lot at the condominium complex where Dylan lived. She appreciated not having to navigate in the dark, but she tilted her head to shield Jimmy's eyes from the glare. He nuzzled his cheek into her collarbone, resettling himself.

Please don't wake up. She'd rather not deal with two fretful children if she could help it. Jimmy had roused briefly when she secured him in his car seat. She'd explained in a singsong tone what was going on, hoping he only heard the lullaby voice, not the details.

"Thanks for coming," Dylan said, stepping back into his condo. "Do you want me to take him?"

Tara shook her head as she entered and located his couch. "Could you dim the brightness or turn the lamp off over here?"

As he did as she asked, she laid Jimmy down, and the boy opened his eyes. She brushed the hair from his forehead. "We're at Mr. Ross's house, honey, like I told you. You rest here while I go see what's wrong with his little girl."

Jimmy nodded, and his eyes drifted closed. With any

luck, he'd sleep through this all until she got him back home. She didn't want him irritable at the Wee Care tomorrow from interrupted sleep, nor did she want him getting his second wind now and being wide-awake for hours. Usually, he slept like a log. She only hoped that pattern held true this evening.

Tara straightened.

"I really appreciate your coming."

Her storehouse of charity closed to this man. At the moment, she felt too aggravated to empathize with him. "I'm only here for Lily."

"I know." He gave her forearm a brief squeeze.

It should have been a formal gesture, like shaking her hand in gratitude. But it felt…personal. She told herself the tingle zipping up her arm was irritation. Maybe hives. She didn't intend to be drawn to him, despite his good looks or sometimes charming nature. All sorts of vile creatures could be alluring. Venus flytraps. Boa constrictors. Jay. Now Dylan Ross.

"This way." Dylan indicated the hallway.

She scowled, ruffled by her response to him. "I'll just follow the sound of crying."

His jaw hardened. "Look, if you don't want to be here, just leave."

"Fine time for you to say that," she threw at him in a furious but quiet voice. "I already woke my son from a sound sleep and got him out of his bed to come over."

"At least your son went to sleep."

She clenched her teeth. So he was having a bad night. She felt sorry for Lily, not him. Pivoting on her heel, she marched down the hall toward the sound of the little girl whose anguish had brought her here.

The little girl who'd stolen part of her heart that afternoon.

It took almost forty minutes to soothe Lily to sleep, tucked in with a frayed Winnie-the-Pooh bear. Tara snapped on a Cinderella night-light then left the door cracked. Her heart ached in her chest, and she felt wrung out.

While she'd rocked Lily, she had time to think. Recalling her early days of parenting Jimmy on her own helped put things in perspective. She needed to cut Dylan some slack.

He sat at a desk with elaborate and mysterious computer components on it. Papers lay across half of the surface, some with detailed mechanical drawings she took to be computer hardware parts.

He looked up as she neared. "She's finally asleep?"

"Yes. Worn down." She glanced at the empty couch. "Where's Jimmy? Don't tell me he woke up."

"No. I put him in my bed about twenty minutes ago. I wasn't sure if he'd roll off the couch. Thanks for settling Lily." He sighed. "She's been like this since before the funeral."

"I'm sorry for your loss." Tara massaged the tightness in the back of her neck.

"It's Lily who feels it most," he said. "I hadn't seen Rose in a long time."

She didn't want to listen to him talk about his ex. The situation hit too close to home for her to be objective. Even though Dylan hadn't known about his child, Tara had to wonder why Lily's mother *hadn't* contacted him about the baby. Had Rose sensed something about Dylan? Had she realized that his playboy ways wouldn't translate well to fatherhood? Tara hadn't chosen to raise Jimmy alone; the decision had been thrust upon her by default. Still, given that Jay had run off, he wouldn't have provided Jimmy much value as a male role model.

She turned to Dylan but couldn't meet his gaze. The late hour, the quiet, and the dim lighting lent the air a loaded charge. Reminded her they were two adults, alone. Reminded her how attractive he was physically and how long it had been since she'd been with a man—a little over four years. No wonder Dylan affected her on a tummy-tingling level. "I should get Jimmy to his own bed."

"I suppose so," Dylan said.

"He's a sound sleeper." She heard herself babble to fill the silence. The silence that had become intimate and adult as Dylan rose to his feet, mere inches away. "I don't want him having a hard day tomorrow."

"Tara."

She watched Dylan's hand inch toward her and braced herself to react. He caressed her arm in what had to be a gesture of gratitude. She did not—would not—read anything more into it, no matter how his hand lingered, no matter how his gaze locked on hers, no matter how he seemed to be bending toward her. No matter how her throat went dry with anticipation.

"Thank you," he said in a low voice. "I can't tell you what it means to me that you came."

"I came for Lily," she reminded them both in a near whisper.

"Of course." He leaned forward and brushed his lips against hers.

For just a second, she allowed the kiss to continue, enjoying it despite herself. He was only saying thanks, after all. There was nothing romantic in his kiss. Forcing herself to step back, she couldn't deny the effect of his warm touch. She really must be deprived of…sleep.

He perched against his desk, confirming her reading of his motive. Casual gratitude. She was an adult. She could handle an almost-impersonal kiss.

"I'll just get my jacket—"

Lily's cry cut off her words. Tara and Dylan rushed down the hall, stopping outside her door, hearing her sob. "I'll go in," Tara whispered.

Dylan nodded, his mouth set in grim resignation, obviously realizing his presence wouldn't help matters.

Tara patted his arm in reassurance. This touching thing was contagious. "It'll get easier once she gets used to being here."

He nodded and turned away.

It took her another half hour to calm Lily, whose incoherent mumblings offered no clue as to how to help her. Tara dragged herself back to the living room, not surprised to see Dylan still at his desk.

"Putting Jimmy in your bed was genius," she said. "At least he's getting a decent night's sleep."

"That's where you should be."

Tara nodded and covered a yawn, not quite paying attention. But realizing what he'd said and what she'd agreed to, she did a double take.

He grinned. "I didn't mean that the way it sounded. Of course, I didn't *not* mean it either. But for now, it's after midnight. You should just lay down with Jimmy. Try to get some sleep."

"I should go home." She glanced down the hallway. "I can't promise Lily will stay asleep, though, and I hate the idea that she'd wake up and find me gone. It might remind her of her mother leaving her, in a sense."

"Stay. Jimmy will get his rest, and he'll feel better if he wakes up and you're beside him."

Another yawn attacked her. "Sorry. Looks like I could really use some sleep."

Not that lying in Dylan's bed, surrounded by his things and his scent, turned out to be conducive to sleep. But eventually, sheer tiredness won out. Tara drifted off, her cheek against smooth percale, her lungs filled with citrus and evergreen, her mind on a seductive journey of its own.

THE ONLY WARNING Tara had the next morning was the sound of running feet across the day care's tile floor. Squatting in front of a lower bookcase, she started to turn.

"Lily," Dylan called.

Lily tackled her in an exuberant hug. They both toppled to the floor.

"Don't knock down Miss Tara," he finished.

The girl withdrew her arms and scrambled away, stopping in a crouch a few feet to the right, her eyes wide and watchful.

"I'm okay," she assured the girl, despite the sharp ache in her elbow. "How about you? Are you okay?"

Lily nodded.

"Good. I'd hate to think I squashed you like modeling clay," she said to make the girl giggle. "Your daddy worries about you."

Dylan shifted on his feet. "I just didn't want her attacking you."

Tara mentally threw up her hands in defeat. She'd been trying to get Lily to see him as protective. But he had a point. Lily should learn restraint. "*Attacking* might be overstating, don't you think?"

"Fine." He turned to Lily. "I'm sorry if I yelled, pumpkin. I was concerned you or Miss Tara might get hurt."

Tara rose and put out a hand to pull Lily up. After a moment's hesitation, the girl grasped it and stood.

"Looks like we mussed you up some," Tara said. She pulled the girl's sweater straight again. "And that hair. I must have tugged it. Can I fix it for you?"

Dylan cleared his throat, looking rumpled himself. "It looked like that when we came in. She won't let me near her with a brush."

"I figured as much, but I was going for tact." She slid him a glance. "I'd hate to think that was your best effort."

"I did put a brush in her backpack."

Tara raised her eyebrows in question.

"For my mom. I wasn't going to rely on your good nature this morning." He cleared his throat. "You snuck out pretty early. I didn't even hear you."

Tara worked at releasing Lily's ponytail from its rubber band without pulling. She hadn't "snuck out" anywhere. She'd very quietly gone home with hardly a glance at Dylan asleep on his couch. Barely noticed his low-hanging jeans or sliding-up T-shirt, exposing tanned skin and curly dark hair low on his stomach. After a night dreaming of him, she'd been anxious to get home, back to her normal surroundings. "I open on Thursdays and I didn't want to wake you that early. Jimmy and I had to change clothes."

To Lily, she said, "Get your brush from your bag, honey, and let's get you tidied up before the other kids get here."

"Thank you," Dylan said as Lily glided from the room.

His words conjured the feel of his lips against hers. She had to get hold of her imagination. She might scorn his casual dating as a lifestyle, but the practice had made him one heck of a kisser. "Don't mention it."

His phone vibrated, and he threw it an irritable look. "I

didn't realize how often this thing rings. When I had all the free time in the world, it wasn't inconvenient."

"Another girlfriend?" Tara tried for sympathy but it came out as sarcasm instead.

He flipped his phone back out and read the display. "A lady I date, yes. It's hard to explain why I can't go out or haven't called."

She held her tongue. He was her boss's son, after all.

"I'll be at home for a while this morning if you need to contact me." He grimaced. "I was afraid to shower in case something happened and I wouldn't hear Lily. I'm installing safety guards on the door and windows once I get home."

"Good thinking."

"After I woke this morning, all sorts of tragic scenarios made me crazy." His gaze slid from hers. "I'm not at all prepared for fatherhood."

Tara placed a hand on his arm for a moment, moved against her will. "You'll get there. One thing at a time. Safety guards are a good first step."

"Sorry. Don't mean to complain." He rubbed a hand down his face. "I guess I'm overwhelmed and overtired."

That made her grin. "Welcome to parenthood."

"This is awkward, but I'm wondering if you'd do me another favor. It's really more of a favor for Lily."

"What is it?"

"Could she stay over at your house tomorrow night?"

"Tomorrow? I guess so. Why?"

"I have a thing. I'd ask you to just watch her until it's over, but it might be late. On the off-chance she falls asleep at your place, I'd hate to, you know, wake her up."

Tara stared at the color rising under his tan. He was going to go have sex. While she babysat.

Why do you care? It irked her, that was all. He'd just gotten home with Lily. Couldn't he put off his sexual urges? God knew Tara had, for far too long.

"What 'thing' do you have to do?" she asked. "A business meeting? Will you be out of town?"

"Oh, no. I'm not going to travel anytime in the near future. As a matter of fact, my mom even cancelled her trip to Europe."

Tara started. Betty had talked about her trip for months, and he'd let her cancel? "You're kidding."

"She did it before we came back from Kansas. I didn't ask her to, but I'm grateful she did."

"That's very…giving of her."

"And selfish of me, right? Is that what you're not saying?"

She shrugged. "It's none of my business."

"That's true." He cleared his throat. "Sorry. I guess I'm a little testy and this is sure as heck no way to ask you for a favor."

She squared off to him, not quite toe to toe, but her stance didn't miss the mark by much. "Try telling me the truth."

"I'm going to a wedding. I made the plans—okay, the date—before I found out about Lily. The lady I'm taking is a bridesmaid in the wedding. It would be awkward for her to go alone."

Tara crossed her arms. "And?"

He sighed. "And it will be a relief for me to get a break."

That, she understood. "Okay. I'll do it."

He smiled. "Really? I figured that last admission would weigh against me."

She gave him a pitying look. "Dylan, all parents need

a break every once in a while. I'm not surprised, with the level of trauma you've been dealing with this past week, that you'd like to get away."

"I owe you."

"Just bring her things to day care tomorrow morning and let me know when you're planning to pick her up Saturday." She had to laugh at the expression on his face. "You didn't just win the lottery. It's one night."

"You have no idea how relieved I am." He leaned near.

Tara jerked backward. "No PDA at the Wee Care."

He laughed and walked off, whistling.

She'd just provided him with the opportunity to have sex. No wonder he was so happy. The question was, why was she so *un*happy?

DYLAN PROPPED HIS FEET on his coffee table late Friday night, pulling off his loosened tie. His condo was heavy with silence. He tilted the beer he held for a long drink, slouching lower into the couch.

Eleven-thirty. Hopefully Tara had gotten Lily to sleep.

He should be with Ann Marie, his date. She'd made it clear she'd welcome his company overnight. That had been his intention. He had the night free. No worries or responsibilities. No strings. Once in her apartment, Ann Marie had been persuasive, and he knew from their past she was an enthusiastic lover. He'd been more shocked than she had when he'd stopped halfway to her bedroom and said he had to go home.

Barley and hops were no substitute for the taste of Ann Marie's kisses in his mouth. He couldn't believe he'd been such an idiot. Why had he rushed home? To what?

Grabbing the remote, he figured he'd watch something on TV. An R-rated movie Lily shouldn't walk in on. Or sports. He'd turn it as loud as he wanted, not having to worry about anyone sleeping—or crying—down the hall.

Because no one was down the hall.

He flicked off the remote and checked his watch. In a little over seven hours he could pick up Lily, see if she'd slept at all. Tara would probably be glad to get the extra child off her hands. She'd probably take a nap.... Dylan squeezed his eyes shut. He didn't need that image in his head.

The TV came back on at his touch. His premium cable movie station was showing a black-and-white version of *Heidi. Heidi?* Seriously? Flick. A rerun of *Little House on the Prairie.* Flick. *Full House.* Flick. Finally, a baseball game. Or, no, a review of the homerun race from over a decade past. Dylan watched as Mark McGwire hit number 60, then 61, then 62. The slugger crossed the plate—and with a huge grin, raised his son in his arms.

Dylan turned off the TV. Even sports couldn't take his mind off Lily.

When morning came, he was dressed and ready to go long before necessary. A predawn run then a trip to the Piggly Wiggly meant he beat the usual Saturday morning grocery shoppers home.

At 7:30 a.m., he tapped his shoe against Tara's door, hands full of doughnuts, milk and coffee. His eagerness to have the door opened made him shift his shoulders, as though he still wore the button-down Oxford and tie from the evening before instead of a T-shirt. He put it down to anxiety over Lily.

Then Tara opened the door wearing a robe and carrying the tantalizing image of lazy mornings spent under the covers, and he knew what had driven him from his bed.

This was so not good.

"I didn't expect you this early." Tara pushed open the screen door, letting him in.

Dylan handed her the box of doughnuts. "Is Lily up yet? Or maybe I should ask if she slept."

"She slept." Tara set the box on her small dinette table and turned without flipping open the box. "How was your night?"

He couldn't decipher her expression, but something lay beneath her words. Maybe Lily had been a handful after all, and he had to take the brunt of Tara's frustration.

"It was nice." No way would he admit it had ended so early. He'd appear ungrateful if he admitted he'd been back home before midnight, the evening a failure. He pulled out his wallet to pay her. "Thanks again for watching Lily. Did she give you any trouble?"

"Not a bit." Tara grimaced but shoved the handful of bills in her robe pocket without looking at them. "She had dinner, we watched a movie and both kids were in bed by nine."

Dylan was agog. "She fell asleep before nine?"

Unheard of. He wanted to be happy about it—was happy, on some level—but Lily behaving so well for a stranger only emphasized his ineptitude. And her animosity for him. It just plain hurt, dammit.

He cleared his throat. "Great."

"I'll get her," Tara said. "I think I heard her stirring. But Dylan, even though she was no problem, I don't want to get into the habit of babysitting for you. I'm around children all day for a living. I want to dedicate my home time to Jimmy."

"Of course. Sure. That makes sense." He felt as though

someone had pushed his life raft farther away from shore—
and he'd caught a tide.

Buck up. He and Lily would come to some understanding. Eventually. "Thanks for last night. Like I said, I'd had
that date arranged for a while, before I knew about Lily. I
didn't want to make my friend go alone, it being last minute
and all. That can be awkward."

Tara crossed her arms. "I'm sure she was appreciative."

"I don't know about that. I had to explain about Lily and
why I wouldn't be calling her for a while. And why I was
going home early."

Now why had he added that?

"You...? Oh." She tucked a silky blond strand of hair
behind her ear, then gestured to the box. "Would you like
some coffee or milk? Since you brought both."

"I've already had two cups of coffee this morning, but
a doughnut sounds good."

"I'll get the children." Tara fled down the hall, the swing
of her yellow terry-cloth robe making him speculate about
the garments—or lack thereof—underneath.

This was *so* not good.

LATER THAT AFTERNOON, Dylan shifted fast-food bags in
his arms, trying to turn the doorknob at his brother's house
without dropping anything. Only after getting a good grip
and being unsuccessful did he realize the door was locked.
Strange. The kids banged in and out of the house so often
that Adam and Anne rarely locked it during the day. Of
course, a new babysitter would be more cautious.

The June temperature had dropped to the high seventies,
kissing the air with the promise of a summer storm. If he
didn't have food bags to juggle, he'd roam around to the

backyard where someone was sure to be playing while the skies stayed clear.

"It's locked," he said unnecessarily to Lily. Talking to her felt like talking to himself, since she seldom answered. Still, he tried, figuring she'd have to get used to him. She glanced in his direction but looked away when he tried to make eye contact. He poked the doorbell, praying he wouldn't wake up the baby.

The door swung open.

"Uncle Dylan!" A small body hit his legs, arms wrapping around them and almost knocking him backward. He tightened his hold on the bags.

"Hey, squirt."

"I'm not Squirt. I'm Caitlyn."

"So you are. I can't tell any of you kids apart."

A gap-toothed grin shot his way as the girl backed up, not buying his tale. He played this game with all the children, pretending not to know which was which since Adam and Anne's brood now numbered eight. After Mary had come the triplets, then Caitlyn, then the twins, and now baby Penny. Hopefully, Adam was done being fruitful and multiplying the earth's population.

"Hi, Lily," Cait said.

"Hi," she whispered back.

"We got comp'ny."

Dylan's eyebrows rose at the term. Adam's household had employed every girl in the town of Howard from age twelve up, usually several at a time. Younger sitters served as helping hands to the more experienced teens. Today his mother had planned to watch the children but was detained. He'd been enlisted to help out whatever new girl had been saddled with the Ross Rascals until she arrived. Other than the night before, he'd spent almost a week listening to his daughter cry herself to sleep. He'd be glad to be around children who liked him.

He and Lily had come for dinner Wednesday night after Lily had spent her first day at the Wee Care. A day she'd spent in Tara's arms or on her lap, according to his mom. While he was grateful Lily had latched onto someone, it rankled that it hadn't been him. Their lives would be easier if Lily could at least tolerate him.

Maybe his daughter recognized something in Tara that reminded her of her own mother. Both women had raised their babies without marrying the kids' fathers. Perhaps that left some kind of aura children could sense. So, although it needled him, he could understand Lily's link with Tara.

"Here, squirt." He handed Cait one of the lighter food bags, the same size as the one Lily carried. "Take this to the kitchen."

"I'm *Caitlyn*."

"Oh, right. Sorry, Caity."

He grinned as she walked off, shaking her head. Going after her, he glanced around, keeping an ear open. He had to turn and check to see if Lily followed him in, she was so quiet. The house seemed normal, neat and cheery, with toys in baskets pushed to the sides of the room to allow for walking. He heard muted music and figured nine-year-old Mary would be dancing in her room.

Setting his and Lily's bags on the kitchen counter, he noticed the dishes in the sink. Someone was shirking his or her duties, taking advantage of the new babysitter. Good thing he'd come.

"Where do you think everyone's got to?" he asked Lily.

She shrugged. She hadn't spoken or looked higher than

his T-shirt, but at least she'd responded. He counted it as a victory.

Movement outside drew him to the kitchen window. A profusion of bubbles blew past, their iridescent rainbows sparkling in the sun. He searched for the source and spotted the three-year-old twins, Brian and Bethany, with another boy around their size, puffing out soapy circles between their giggles.

Dylan frowned, trying to place the extra child. The kid faced away, but something about him looked familiar. With a snort of laughter, Dylan considered that maybe he wasn't kidding Caitlyn, after all. Had he forgotten one of his nephews? While he watched the three-month-old, Penny, opening and closing her chubby hands as she lay in her carrier in the shade, the boy turned. Jimmy Montgomery.

His gaze flew across the yard, zeroing in on Tara with Mary and the six-year-old triplets forming a conga line. Their laughter lilted on the air, overriding the music. Caitlyn had obviously run through the house to join the others, and she now climbed on the wooden play set Adam had built.

Sunlight gleamed through Tara's shoulder-length silver-blond hair. She laughed, easy and joyful, like one of the kids. He could rationalize the pull he felt. Any man would appreciate her beauty, like admiring a living work of art, but her attraction ended at the physical for him. Not only did she not seem to care for him for some reason, but when he looked at Tara, he thought of Rose and all she'd deprived him of with Lily. He recognized his attitude as unfair; he just couldn't seem to shake it.

The dance line veered off to weave through five of the tall orange plastic construction cones the kids used for play. Caitlyn joined them as they ducked under the trapeze bar on the play set. When they jumped over a broomstick set on cardboard boxes, Dylan realized the dancers had journeyed through an obstacle course.

The music paused then played "Head and Shoulders, Knees and Toes," making Dylan groan. He'd never mastered the moves, which made his nieces and nephews laugh and heckle him. All the kids, including the bubble blowers, started dancing.

He waited until the song stopped before venturing out, with Lily silent alongside him. He didn't want the kids taunting him to try to join in. His daughter didn't think much of him as it was; he didn't need her to know he couldn't manage simple dance movements.

A squeal alerted him just before his knees were hit from behind, once again nearly toppling him. Brian jumped up and down near his feet.

"Uncle Dywin!" Brian's twin, Bethany, stretched her arms toward him in the universal "pick me up" gesture, straining on tiptoe to get his attention. He swung her into his arms, then grabbed up Brian for a hug, too. His gaze met Tara's as she crossed the yard. Lily rushed to her side.

"Your mom said she'd call in the cavalry to help me," Tara said, giving Lily a one-armed embrace, "but I didn't expect you."

"Hi. Hey, kids," he called to the rest of them, returning their greetings as they approached. "I brought food, but I guess you've eaten."

Mary appeared at his side as the twins slid to the ground. "We had spaghetti."

He nodded.

"It was all I could think of," Tara said, "that was fast, filling, kid-friendly, and easy to make a lot of."

"I asked for pizza," Mary said in a sulky tone.

"Pizza," Christopher, the wild six-year-old triplet, exhaled the word with longing.

"Sorry," Tara told them. "I didn't want to turn on the oven with nine children to tend to."

Dylan scowled at the kids. "Hey. Did you eat?"

They all nodded.

"Then be grateful you got food at all." He eyed the triplets. "Are you supposed to clean up the dishes this week?"

Paul, Christopher and Jane nodded.

"I cleared the table," Jane reported. "Paul scrubbed the plates and rinsed the milk out of the glasses."

She looked at Christopher, who hung his head.

"I told them to come outside," Tara broke in. "It isn't his fault the dishes aren't in the dishwasher."

Chris beamed at her, avoiding his uncle's eye.

"But maybe we should go in and get that done," Tara added, reaching down to touch her son's shoulder. "We could all use a drink to cool down."

"We don't got to go inside for that," Caitlyn said. She ran to the back wall of the house.

"Cait," Dylan called. "Hold on."

She twisted the water faucet with both hands then grabbed up the hose.

"Not Cait," she called. "Squirt."

And she aimed the hose at Dylan.

Chapter Four

The kids squealed, running from the spray.

Tara watched them scatter, distancing herself from Dylan, who took the brunt of the shower. His stern, narrow-eyed countenance didn't bode well for Caitlyn.

"You'd best turn off that water." He locked gazes with the girl.

She shot him full in the chest, laughing. Tara gasped and darted a worried glance at Dylan. A hand fisted in the leg of her shorts. She wasn't surprised to see Lily at her side.

"Caitlyn," the oldest girl yelled. "Drop the hose."

"Don't do it, Cait," Christopher argued, darting away from a blast of water as she turned in his direction. "It's all you got."

"Hey, boy." Dylan glowered at him. "When I'm done with her, you're next."

Chris laughed and ran to the play set on the farther side of the yard.

Tara saw the water arcing her way as Caitlyn turned again. She pushed Lily behind her just as a cold stream pelted her before moving on. Tara straightened and shook back her hair. The three-year-old twins and Jimmy ran under and through the arch of water as though it were high summer rather than humid and close, with the threat of an impending storm. The baby lay asleep in her carrier in the shade, out of harm's way.

Tara turned back to Caitlyn and Dylan, wondering how best to proceed. How strict was he? As their uncle, he had more authority here, but his general incompetence at fatherhood made her hesitate to trust him.

"This is your last warning, Caity." Dylan crossed his arms.

She sprayed him in the face. Tara caught her breath in apprehension but the kids fell about the yard, holding their stomachs with laughter.

Dylan stalked toward Caitlyn, rubbing one hand over his face and holding the other out to ward off the spray. Caitlyn scooted sideways. With a lunge, Dylan grabbed the hose from her hands.

Tara frowned in confusion. The children continued laughing, so she halted her instinctive step forward.

"No, Uncle Dylan!" the girl shrieked.

"Too bad you didn't think about consequences sooner, young lady."

And he doused her with water.

The kids called out to her, either encouraging Cait to make a run for it or for their Uncle Dylan to "soak her good."

Tara laughed, relieved he had a sense of humor. She caught sight of Jimmy, standing stock-still, watching with his mouth open, the only one other than Penny and Lily not laughing now. Being an only child, he was probably confused by the proceedings. Tara admitted to feeling the same. The Ross household reminded her of a circus. Wild and bizarre, but fun.

Dylan put an arm around Caitlyn's stomach and lifted

her off her feet. He dropped the hose and turned off the faucet.

"Now you're gonna get it," one of the boys called.

"You certainly are," Dylan said. He tickled her belly.

"No!" Cait gasped through her laughter. "Stop."

"Say 'uncle,'" her oldest sister advised, inching closer.

"It's too late for 'uncle,'" Dylan said. "Her uncle has no mercy."

Caitlyn pushed at his hands as he tickled her armpit. "Not there."

"Take off her shoes," shouted Christopher, the incorrigible triplet. "She's really ticklish on her feet."

Dylan stopped and slid Caitlyn to the ground. He turned to the boy. "And just where are you ticklish?"

Chris ran across the yard with Dylan following close behind, purposely not quite catching him as he darted this way and that. The twins and other two triplets took up the chase, staying behind Dylan. Even Caitlyn joined in.

At least the run would dry everyone out.

Except Jimmy, Tara realized. He stood avidly watching the action. She knelt beside him, Lily at her side.

"Is that man mad?" he asked.

"Nope." Maybe crazy, she thought, but not angry, which was what worried her son. "It's all a game."

Jimmy turned to her. "So I could go run, too?"

She patted his arm. "Sure."

He took off, galloping near the twins, Bethany and Brian, who attended the Wee Care with him.

She and Lily walked over to the oldest girl, who hovered near the tree with longing on her face. Tara could almost see the conflict in her mind, debating whether she should give up her nine-year-old dignity or miss out on the fun. "If you ran after them, you could catch up."

Mary shrugged. "Uncle Dylan will catch Chris and tickle him, too."

Her prediction came just then. Dylan tackled the boy and started in as the others piled on. The kids began tickling one another and Dylan.

"Uncle," he called, making them laugh harder. He rose, pulling some of the smaller children up with him.

"Shall we get that drink now?" Tara asked as Dylan drew near.

"I've had enough water, thank you," he said.

They all laughed, while Caitlyn grinned with pride. Tara wished he didn't look so huggable. Huggable men were off the menu till after the custody hearing, at the very least. Dylan Ross would never make it on her list. He had too many negative checkmarks, despite his skill as an uncle.

"But I could use some lemonade, if there is any." He grabbed Penny's carrier and led the way in like the Pied Piper, with nine kids and one bemused woman trailing behind.

How could he be so good with his nieces and nephews but have no clue how to connect with his own child? Of course, there were huge differences between the two roles. An uncle got to go home to peace and quiet, while parenting duties never ended.

"Let's get dried off first," Tara decided, "then we'll get some drinks."

"But I'm *thirsty*," Christopher croaked dramatically, holding his throat with both hands.

Dylan caught his eye, and the boy subsided. Tara suppressed a smile. Had Dylan, the boy terror, once been as cute and spirited as Christopher? Dylan deposited the baby carrier on the floor and instructed two of the children to retrieve towels from the adjacent laundry room. Chris climbed onto the counter and handed plastic cups down to Caitlyn. One child opened the refrigerator door, and Dylan lifted the heavy pitcher. The Rosses worked like a well-tuned machine. Impressed, but with nothing to do, Tara pulled up a chair. Lily sank to the floor beside her.

Someone dropped a pile of towels on the table. Dylan pulled out a chair opposite her and called the twins. Tara grabbed a towel and rubbed Brian's head, glad the boys' short haircuts would help them dry quickly. Their run around the yard left Brian damp, although no longer dripping.

Dylan peeked under the towel he held and smiled at Bethany, revealing her messy shoulder-length brown hair. "Get me your comb, kiddo, and we'll see about those tangles."

"Okay." She scampered off.

He grabbed the body nearest him, which happened to be Jimmy. Tara tensed.

"Hey," Dylan said with feigned surprise. "You don't look like a rascally Ross. How come you got soaked?"

"Caitlyn sprayed everyone," her son replied solemnly.

"So she did. I'm their uncle Dylan. You've mostly been asleep when I've been around. Do you remember me?"

The boy nodded.

"Nice to meet you again." Dylan threw the towel over her son's blond head and rubbed gently. "Sorry you got caught in the cross fire."

"The what?"

Dylan chuckled. "Got wet for no reason."

Jimmy tented the front of the towel with two hands to stare out. "All us but Lily got wet, even Mom."

Dylan studied Tara for a long moment.

She wished she'd tended to her own appearance before

working on the kids. Drowned Rat wasn't in fashion this year. Although why his opinion would even register on her radar baffled her.

Bethany rushed in with a pink wide-toothed comb. Dylan took it and steadied her between his knees.

She turned huge brown eyes to him. "Don't puw it."

"I won't. You let me know if it hurts, okay?" He kissed the top of her head.

Tara continued to watch Dylan, trying to figure him out.

"Can you do mine, please?" Jane, the girl triplet, asked quietly at Tara's side, drawing her gaze from the contradictory man across from her. Tara nodded. Jane handed over her hairbrush and turned her back to Tara, valiantly entrusting her with the task. Tara separated knots with her fingers, determined to live up to the shy girl's faith. Not only did the girl's hair resemble dark golden sand, it clumped like wet sand, too.

From the corner of her eye, Tara noticed Lily pull her ponytail over her shoulder and begin untangling it with her fingers. Dylan seemed gentle enough combing Bethany's hair. Lily's topknot had been pulled through a rubber band and had snarly strands poking out. Unless he cut the band out at night, hopefully without cutting any hair in the process, removing it would be painful and damaging.

Dylan's cell phone rang. He glanced at the display. "Not my mom," he told Tara. He put the phone back in the pocket of his shorts.

"I can take care of the kids if you need to call your girlfriend or whoever."

Dylan shook his head. "I don't have a girlfriend, and I can call Cherise back later."

"Why limit yourself to just one woman, after all?" Tara

tried for nonchalance, but his attitude annoyed her. He had to be around thirty. Wasn't it time to grow up?

Dylan narrowed his eyes but said nothing.

The oldest girl pulled a comb through her own dark blond hair while a straggly-haired Cait rocked the baby's carrier. Tara finished Jane's hair and smiled in response to the girl's quiet thanks. "Can you loan me a ponytail holder for Lily?"

Jane's gaze flickered to her cousin on the floor before she nodded and darted from the room. When she returned, she bent in front of Lily, her manner tentative, like one approaching a wild doe. "Do you want to borrow my brush?"

Lily took the brush and looked up at Tara. Without speaking, she expressed her need with those brilliant green eyes. Did she think Tara would refuse? Tara nodded and considered the girl in front of her. Jane held out the scissors she'd brought along.

"It's the best way." Jane took Lily's hand. "Miss Tara's going to cut the rubber band out, but she'll be careful. She didn't pull my hair even one time."

Lily nodded and squeezed her eyes shut, her small hand going white around Jane's.

Tara caught Dylan's gaze and registered the dark look before he turned away. His jaw tensed.

She snipped the band and gently peeled it from the entangled strands. Jane's breath whooshed out before she smiled at her cousin.

Dylan continued talking to the boys, and Tara realized he'd stopped to watch them. She ran her fingers through Lily's long hair first then brushed it into a princess braid

"I like that," Mary said, surprising Tara. The girl hadn't warmed up to Tara all day and had hardly spoken. "It's easier than a French braid, the way you just flipped it around her face."

"I like it, too," Jane said. She squatted to Lily's eye level. "It's very pretty."

Lily's gaze darted between her cousins then up to Tara for confirmation. Tara nodded. "Very pretty."

"Thanks," Lily whispered to all three.

Tara rose and poured out the lemonade. She handed Dylan his glass.

"So, Christopher," he said, "don't you have something to do?"

"Yes, sir." Chris crossed the room and opened the dishwasher. The other triplets rose to help, handing him a plate from the sink and lifting the little ones to the faucet so they could rinse their cups themselves.

Tara smiled as one triplet helped the other without being asked. She caught Dylan's look of pride.

"They're good kids," he said.

"I can tell. You should be proud."

"I didn't have anything to do with it. Their parents—" he leaned forward and dropped his voice "—beat it into them."

She gave him a slight smile but reminded herself of his philandering ways in order to counteract the effect of his charm.

"Or they taught them by example," he said, shrugging. "Believe whichever story you prefer."

"Sorry, not buying it. I can feel the love in this house."

"I finished," Christopher called. "Can we watch a movie?"

Dylan caught Tara's eye. "Your call. I'm just backup."

"Everyone pick up the yard first."

"I'll help put away the bubbles." Jane turned to the younger children. "Can you help me find the wands?"

Jimmy trotted after Bethany and Brian, ready to do his part. Tara grinned, guilty of pride herself. Although not used to the group dynamic, he'd caught on and jumped in to help. Lily stood just outside the doorway, not easy with either faction, adult or child.

Cait grabbed Lily's hand and tugged. "You can come with me. You don't got to help, though, 'cause you didn't get to play."

Penny slept on in her carrier, emphasizing the sudden quiet as the other children left them alone.

Tara cleared her throat and moved a step away from Dylan. "So, when did your mom think she'd get here?"

"I'm not sure." He frowned. "Come to think of it, she seemed evasive about just what had delayed her."

"I don't remember any meeting she had for the Wee Care today. It must be something personal."

"Strange." He shook himself. "But I don't want you to have to babysit on your day off."

She narrowed her eyes at his taunt.

"I can take care of the kids for the rest of the afternoon. Maybe being here with the others would be good for Lily."

"No, I promised I'd stay. And Jimmy's having fun."

"You don't have a boyfriend waiting for you?"

She sensed an underlying tone. The way he avoided her gaze made her suspicious of hidden meaning. "No, I don't. Just because I'm a single mom doesn't mean I'm easy."

"Believe me, I have never associated the word *easy* with anything about you."

Tara bit back a smile. She knew better than to be beguiled by him, but she couldn't sustain her anger with him, either.

"Then, as there's no boyfriend to rip my head off for asking, would you go out to dinner with me?"

Her eyes widened. "Oh."

Dylan mentally grimaced as she quickly backpedaled, physically and mentally, he'd guess, and checked on Penny. His impetuous idea would be hard enough to phrase without factoring in her resistance to him. It wasn't as though he wanted to date her, just pick her brain.

"If you don't want to, it's okay." He almost hoped she would refuse. His life had enough complications at the moment.

Tara peeked over her shoulder at him before straightening a wrinkle in Penny's onesie. Her hands caressed the baby, who slept peacefully and didn't need soothing. Dylan recognized the move as a way of centering herself. He'd seen Anne do the same thing with the kids, drawing on their innocence and serenity to find her own calm.

Dylan rolled his eyes. When had he last stumbled over asking a woman out to dinner? Probably in his teens. "Hey, don't sweat it. Let's forget I asked."

She blinked. "You've already changed your mind?"

"No. I mean, yes. Look, I'm not asking you for a date. I'm sorry if you misunderstood. I hoped you could offer me some parenting advice." He ran a hand across the back of his neck. "I thought I'd adjust better to fatherhood, having so much experience with Adam and Anne's kids. It's different with Lily. *She's* different."

Tara picked a piece of grass off the side of the carrier.

"But if going out with me makes you uncomfortable, forget it. It doesn't matter." Which was a patent lie, and they both knew it. As a father, Dylan's efforts fell short.

Since Lily hadn't connected with his mom, he had no one but Tara to turn to for advice. "I just thought you'd help me, for Lily's sake."

She smoothed Penny's almost invisible, baby-fine blond hair, still not meeting his eye. "I don't know what I could tell you that would help. Lily's grieving. She's lost her mother, been taken from her home and made to live with a stranger."

"I'm her father."

"That's just a word to Lily. You haven't been in her life till now."

He clenched his jaw and looked away. *Dammit.* He would have been, had he known about his daughter. But that hardly helped either of them now. As much as he hated to admit it, he was as alien a creature to his little girl as if he'd come from Jupiter.

Dylan swallowed his pride. "Maybe you could help with the basics then. Obviously I stink at hairdos. I probably would have ripped out half her hair removing that rubber band. Just imagine how that would have endeared me to Lily."

Tara opened her mouth, then paused. "I wondered why you were glaring at us."

"Glaring? I didn't mean to. Watching you brought home to me all the simple stuff I don't know, like don't use rubber bands for ponytails."

She sighed. "Okay, I'll go to dinner with you."

Joan of Arc had probably shown the same enthusiasm as she'd climbed onto her pyre of wood.

WHAT WAS I THINKING? Tara put her hands on her hips and stared into the abyss of her closet. Dylan had looked so desperate, and then he'd seen her reluctance and had tried to ease her way out. Not that she didn't have excuses enough to refuse him; she just hadn't used them.

For starters, she hadn't gone on a date in over four years. The last time she'd been with a guy, she'd told him he was about to become a father. Which had also been the last time she'd seen Jamison Albert Summerfield III. Jay had boarded the first plane out of the country, winding up in Portugal.

She also had nothing to wear, which was obvious as she perused her choices. "Dinner" could mean anything. In her world, dinner out meant Mickey D's. In the world of normal grown-ups like Dylan, it could be a thirty-minute drive into Kansas City for a steak at an expensive restaurant or barbecue or Thai. Her stomach growled as she thought of the possibilities.

Even though she'd brought her clothes with her when she'd left home and most of them still fit, those were princess clothes, and she had no intention of going back to that lifestyle. These days she lived in jeans and a sweatshirt or shorts and a T-shirt. If he'd had time to make plans or even think the thing through, Dylan could have given her a hint of their destination so she'd know what to wear.

Of course, she thought with a wry smile, if he'd thought the thing through, he wouldn't have asked her in the first place. The butterflies in her stomach had little to do with clothes and a lot to do with the reluctant attraction she felt for Dylan Ross.

Not that she planned to act on it. She couldn't become involved with a man right now, so it was a darn good thing he just wanted advice. If at times she yearned for affection from a male over three years old, she told herself she'd work that in later along the road. She'd date again, but not a playboy like Dylan. Perhaps after she'd finished her education degree, she'd find someone she could love and believe in. Someone who'd love her and her son. Someone she'd value as a role model for Jimmy.

None of which included Dylan Ross.

Those plans were set far in the future, regardless of how her stubborn hormones shrieked every time he entered the room.

An hour later, sixteen-year-old Kim from the adjoining duplex sat in the front room with Jimmy. Tara had decided on black slacks and a lilac silk blouse, which had been comfortably elegant in Rome four years before but now looked drab. However, it should fit in whether they went casual or semi-dressy.

The doorbell rang. The butterflies in her stomach morphed into pelicans.

Dylan stood outside the door with Lily just behind him.

"Sorry," he said. "I couldn't call you with little ears listening, so I just came by."

Lily rushed forward and hugged Tara.

Tara patted her and eased her away. "Hey, sweetie, it's good to see you, too. Jimmy's in his room. Go say hi."

With a backward glance, Lily left them at the door.

"Kim," Tara called to her babysitter. "I'm going to step outside with Mr. Ross for a minute."

The teen nodded.

"What's going on?"

"Lily burst into tears when she realized I planned to leave her at Adam's, even with all her cousins and her grandma there. Caity has made Lily her special friend, but Lily hasn't taken to her with the same enthusiasm." Dylan ran a hand through his hair. "Poor Caity looked ready to burst into tears herself when Lily insisted on leaving. I couldn't even be happy she'd chosen me for a change."

"Maybe another time then."

He paid Kim, ignoring Tara's protests and Kim's assertions that she didn't need payment for work she didn't do. Then he watched from Tara's porch until the teen passed the bushes separating their doorways and entered her family's half of the duplex.

Blowing out a breath, he turned to find three upturned faces, as the kids had joined Tara in the front room. As much as he wanted—needed—Tara's advice, he couldn't get it with his daughter around.

"Well, we've said hello," he told his daughter.

"Thanks for stopping by," Tara said. "I'll see you at school, Lily."

Dylan appreciated her playing along, as though a brief visit had always been the plan.

BUT SHE SAW LILY long before school. In fact, it was only hours later that she walked into Dylan's condo with Jimmy by her side.

"I'm sorry. Did my call wake him up?"

Tara nodded, but she appeared resigned rather than angry. "Is Lily still throwing up?"

"Not in the past twenty minutes." He grimaced. "She won't let me near her. No surprise there, but I haven't been able to clean her up or change her pajamas. I tried and she shrieked like a banshee."

Tara left him to settle Jimmy in his bed while she went through the process of calming Lily, this time adding a bath and fresh pajamas to the ritual because of the vomit.

Dylan ran a hand through his hair, frustrated at his own

failure. There had to be a better solution. How could he stop taking Jimmy out of bed but still get Tara here for Lily?

By the time Tara entered the living room half an hour later, he'd come up with a plan. Maybe he'd gone crazy from lack of sleep and too much worry, and maybe this was the trickiest water he'd submerged himself into in a long time, but he felt more in control having figured out a solution. No matter how far-fetched.

He wished he'd had a stiff whiskey or something while Tara had been down the hall with Lily. A little Dutch courage would go a long way. However, he'd have to do his best with the daring he had.

"Thank you," he said when she entered the living room. "I'm sorry for all the repeated phone calls. For dragging Jimmy out of his bed." He tried on a smile. "But I think I have a solution."

Her eyebrows rose in question, doubt evident on her face.

"Tara, I have a proposition, uh, of sorts, for you." *Poor choice of words, Ross.* Because he could see taking Tara to bed, despite their lack of agreement on most issues. They had an uneasy truce for the most part, which would make his next words insane. But, for Lily, he'd do anything. Even this.

She'd locked her teeth together, probably to keep from telling him where he could stick *that* kind of proposition. Her face had gone pink, no doubt from outrage. Dylan took a deep breath, wishing for his oxygen tank. He was about to plunge into deep and dangerous waters.

"I'd like for you to move in here. As my nanny," Dylan added quickly.

Tara shook her head, staring as though he'd lost his mind. He probably had.

"I know it's crazy. You and I don't get along all that well." *The understatement of the year.* "But this is for Lily. I can't call you every night, expecting you to wake Jimmy just to get Lily to sleep. It's not fair to you or him."

"I can't."

"Unfortunately, I haven't seen any improvement," he continued, ignoring her. Maybe if he just kept talking, he'd wear her down. "I'm at my wit's end trying to take care of her. Even though she's at day care when I'm at work, there's all the rest of the time. Neither of us is sleeping."

He shook his head. "I try to read to her every night, thinking if we got into a routine, she'd relax a little."

"That's an excellent idea."

"But she doesn't warm up, no matter what I do." He held her gaze. "Not like she does with you."

"Dylan, I sympathize with your problem, but I can't just uproot Jimmy from his home. Besides, the timing is crazy for me."

"I know it wouldn't be easy for you or Jimmy to move. But I'll be paying for all the food, too, and you can save money for college. Mom says you're going to be a teacher. Maybe you could rent out your place for…" He trailed off. *Crap.*

She smirked. "Ah. Now reality hits. How long were you going to hire me for? Just until Lily settles in? That's not real fair."

"Let's say six months, even if Lily settles in sooner." He nodded decisively. "That'll get her into kindergarten and through her first holidays without Rose. After that, we can reassess the situation, see how Lily's doing, how you and I and Jimmy are handling it, and decide then if you need or want to stay on."

"I can't see how this would work, and it's impossible for me anyway."

"My condo has two spare rooms. Lily's using the guest bedroom now, and the other room is basically storage, but I can clean it out."

"Oh, for Pete's sakes, Dylan. Listen to yourself."

"Moving is already on my to-do list. We need a bigger place. I've checked, and a unit with four bedrooms comes available in a month."

"A month? You may not need me in a month. And why are you moving into a place with four bedrooms?"

"I'm going to hire live-in help. I need a room for the nanny, my bedroom, Lily's bedroom, and either an office for me or playroom for her. She can't be playing in the same place I'm working."

"So you're getting a nanny anyway?"

"I have to travel on-site sometimes to troubleshoot the programs and hardware we sell. Someone will need to be here for Lily in the night and to pick her up after school when I'm at work. She could go to the Wee Care, but I'll still need a backup plan, and I don't want to put the responsibility on my mom. So I'll have to move anyway."

"And what do you plan to do for the next month? Call me every night?" She stopped.

He grinned, glad she understood his point. Moving in meant Jimmy wouldn't have to be taken from his bed.

"Not that I'm even considering this insane idea."

But she was, he could tell. For the first time since he'd conceived the idea—another poor turn of phrase—he felt hopeful. "I'll sleep on the couch for now. You can have my room." He blocked out the image of her in his bed, rumpled and warm, tangled in his sheets. He cleared his throat. "Jimmy will have his own room. He can bring all his stuff from your house."

She rubbed her temple. "You make it sound so plausible."

"It is. I know it could work." He took both her hands in his. "Tara, I'll be forever in your debt. There's no better start for a friendship between us than our children's interests. You're fond of Lily, and Jimmy would have her as a live-in playmate, plus all Adam's kids."

She hesitated. "I didn't want to discuss my personal problems, but you deserve to know why I have to turn you down. It isn't because I don't care about Lily. If I could help you, I'd seriously think about doing this."

"Okay." He led her to the couch and sat beside her, ready to talk her around to his point of view. "So what is it?"

"I'm being sued for custody of Jimmy."

He felt his eyes go wide, then his jaw tightened. "His dad?"

Tara grimaced. "Close. His dad's parents."

"Why?" He shook his head. "I can't imagine that. You're such a good mother."

"My situation isn't like yours. Even my parents are sympathetic to the Summerfields. They were best friends. The rich travel together and live in a pretty insular world. My family's not supportive the way yours is."

"God." He ran a hand over his face. "I feel like a jerk, only thinking of my problems."

"You're thinking of Lily. That's commendable. You need to do right by her just as I need to do what's best for Jimmy."

"You didn't say why they would do this."

Tara dropped her gaze. "I'm not sure. I haven't seen them

in years. Maybe they believe their money will provide a better home for Jimmy."

"Is there a chance these people will win?"

She clasped her hands to her stomach, looking sick with dread. "Money means a good lawyer, and they can provide a two-parent home."

"But they can't love him more than you."

"I know. They don't even know him."

"How much contact have they had with Jimmy?"

She squeezed her eyes shut for a moment. "None."

"Well, that says something right there. You'd think they'd have wanted to be around when he was a baby."

"You'd think so, yes."

Her answers sounded evasive. Something nagged at the back of his brain, but Dylan couldn't pin it down. What wasn't she telling him?

"On the positive side," she said, "I'm young, whereas Albert just turned sixty-seven and Marnie's nearly that. So I've got age and energy to my credit, but no husband, no education, no fortune." She buried her face in her hands. "I'm so screwed."

"Not necessarily. Let's try to think of solutions."

Tara shook her head. "I wish I could help you, really. If I moved in here and rented out my half of the duplex, I could use that money and the nanny salary to pay for a better lawyer. Unfortunately, moving in with you would make me look loose, irresponsible and not much different from the wild teenager Jay's parents remember. I wouldn't want a person like that raising my child, either."

"Whatever you were like as a teenager shouldn't be counted against you now."

"I'm really sorry. I know you were hoping for my help."

"Don't be sorry. You have to do what's best for Jimmy. Let's think rationally."

He crossed his arms and leaned back against the couch. "Tell me the reasons you think they could win."

"They have money."

"You're his mother. Surely that counts heavily in your favor."

"I've been reading up. The courts are deciding more in favor of grandparents in custody cases."

"What other charges, or whatever they're called, can they bring against you?"

"They think I'm an unfit parent because I was a crazy, out-of-control teenager. They don't know how I've changed."

"That's all they've got?"

She looped her hair behind her ears. "They also could argue I don't have their amount of money, which is true, or a college education to get a higher-paying job, which is also true. And any better job I get would take away from my time with Jimmy, plus the salary would go toward day care and sitters instead of improving our situation."

"Which is why you obtained a position at the day care that would allow you to be with him and earn money at the same time."

"I appreciate you seeing my side. I'm worried, Dylan." She traced a circle on the coffee table. "A lot of grandparents raise children these days, but they have to. The parents leave or take drugs. Jimmy has me."

"So the main problem is you can't provide a father," Dylan said.

"Or loads of money." Tara sighed. "I'll have my lawyer argue against Albert Summerfield's age. Sixty-seven isn't old, unless you're chasing after a toddler. He might not be able to play with Jimmy or keep up with his activities. Maybe we'll point out Albert will need to be driving to his doctor rather than coaching soccer."

He stared at her for a minute. "Or you could provide Jimmy with a father."

"Very funny."

"I'm serious." Dylan took her hands in his. "Marry me."

Chapter Five

His words stunned Tara like a Taser shot. "That's not funny."

"I didn't mean it to be funny," Dylan said. "Let me help you while you help me with Lily."

She snatched her hands away. "Be serious. We…we barely know each other."

"It would be like one of those old-time arranged marriages, only we do the arranging ourselves. It works out for both of us. You get a two-parent home, and I get a nanny Lily trusts."

Tara stared at him. "You *are* serious."

He nodded, looking deceptively sane.

"What about after the court case? After Lily gets settled?"

"We'll get a divorce. With no hard feelings because we know where we stand from the start."

She glared at him. "You mean we'd get an annulment."

After a minute he said, "Sure, an annulment. Right. No sleeping together, of course."

"It wouldn't be a real marriage so we wouldn't be doing that." She put her hands to her temples. "Which is stupid to even talk about, since I'm not agreeing to this crazy scheme."

"Jimmy gets a dad. You get a two-parent home with a two-parent income and the semblance of stability for the case. It's not crazy."

"And Lily?"

"Lily benefits, as well. She gets settled and into kindergarten. That would give you time to mend fences with your in-laws."

"I wasn't married to Jay, so they're not officially my in-laws, ex or otherwise. He didn't want to marry me just because he'd used a faulty condom."

"Then he's a jerk. We don't want them to try this later on when our marriage regrettably falls apart."

"Our rather hasty marriage," she pointed out. "That's not going to make me look very responsible. We haven't known one another long enough to have fallen in love."

He winked. "I'll swear I'm devoted to you, which I am. Perhaps you don't know what you've come to mean to me because of Lily."

Tara melted a little inside. She understood, since she had a soft spot for anyone who wanted to protect Jimmy. Right now, that included Dylan. "I don't know. It's impulsive."

"It's a win-win."

Tara shook her head. Men. So damned logical and so totally clueless. "But what about Lily's well-being? When we get our annulment, she'll lose another mother figure."

Dylan raked a hand through his hair and paced. After a moment, he stopped in front of Tara. "We'll have to tell the kids, I guess."

She gawked. "Tell them what?"

"That we're only getting married for a while, but it's a

secret." He shook his head. "Let's not borrow trouble, okay? Think about my proposal. We'll work out the rest later."

Jay's parents had a chance at winning, but she had reason on her side. The case would probably never go before a judge in the first place. Surely their attorney had drafted that letter as a bluff, trying to get her to fall into line?

So why didn't she just flat-out tell Dylan no?

Because she couldn't take any risks with the case. What if having a husband *would* sway the judge in her favor?

Or probably because she cared so much for Lily. That was it.

She tossed and turned in Dylan's bed, staring at Jimmy's silhouette snuggled beside her and wondering how the arrangement would affect him. By morning she was no closer to agreeing, but she hadn't dismissed the idea, either.

Having a man in the picture as a role model, financial help and the facade of a stable home life might make a difference. If only she knew whether this would aid or cripple her chances in the hearing.

Breakfast was leisurely as neither adult had to rush to work on a Sunday. Missing church after such a sleepless night made sense. Checking Lily's forehead with a kiss, Tara didn't notice any fever. The girl's skin wasn't any paler than usual, her eyes were clear and her spirit chipper. Thankfully, last night's vomiting had stemmed from emotional upset rather than a virus—if one could be thankful about such an option.

"Good morning," Dylan said over his shoulder as she wandered in for breakfast. He flipped silver-dollar-size pancakes at the stove.

"Why do I smell gravy? And biscuits?"

"Maybe because I'm making biscuits and gravy?

And scrambled eggs. I didn't know what you like for breakfast."

The twinkle in his eye made her wonder how many women he served breakfast to after a night of lovemaking. He was skilled in the kitchen, and she'd just bet—

"How did you sleep?"

"Sleep?" A yawn overtook her at the thought of burrowing back into the covers.

"Not too well, huh?"

"No, I slept some. I just, you know, have a lot on my mind."

"We can help each other, Tara," Dylan said in a low voice, leaning toward her. "You need time to go to college. I could watch Jimmy at night while you do that."

Surprise arrowed into her. Talk about out of the blue. "I'm so worried about the custody hearing, I've barely thought about anything *other* than marrying you. I'm not coming up with a less crazy solution."

He grinned. "Gee, thanks."

"You know what I mean."

"I do."

Their eyes met and they laughed.

"Have some breakfast," he said as the oven timer dinged. "Things will sound less impossible on a full stomach."

They gathered around the table—fluffy yellow eggs, melt-in-the-mouth biscuits, sausage gravy, and pancakes with the steam rising off them—and four tentative strangers who might become a family. For a while. Tara eyed Dylan as butter melted and slid across her pancake. He could cook. That certainly counted in his favor.

"Pass the syrup, please, Mr. Ross," Jimmy said.

Dylan nodded as he did so. "You have very polite manners."

Jimmy beamed under the male approval as he coated his pancakes with sugary liquid. "I got a wiggly tooth."

She did a double take. He'd told Dylan before telling her?

"That's cool," Dylan said. "Maybe it'll fall out here and the tooth fairy will find you."

Jimmy grasped his front bicuspid between his thumb and forefinger and gave it a tug.

Tara shuddered as his movement made her queasy. "Jimmy, don't do that at the table."

"Did you lose a tooth here?" her son asked Lily.

Lily shook her head then whispered, "At home I did."

Jimmy's face scrunched up as he turned back to Dylan. "How does the tooth fairy know Lily's here now?"

Dylan glanced at Tara.

She fielded the question since her son had asked, and hoped what she said would match Dylan's version. "The tooth fairy knows when a tooth is about to fall out. She can find the child who's going to lose it so she can trade the tooth for something else the child wants."

"I think the family who lived here before me had kids," Dylan added, "so she's probably watching this place, but I haven't lost a tooth for a long time."

Jimmy chortled. "You're silly."

Tara could scarcely believe that this child, so confident with an adult, able to tease a man he barely knew, was her son. He was usually bashful when making a new acquaintance, and adults had to earn his trust. Yet here he sat, with a serious case of hero worship.

Jimmy gulped some milk as a chaser to his mouthful of pancake. "Tommy Ayrens said the tooth fairy brought him five dollars for his tooth."

"Wow." Dylan glanced at Tara. "Is that what teeth are

going for these days? I thought the tooth fairy just brought a new toothbrush."

Both children stopped eating mid-forkful, their appalled expressions forcing Tara to bite her lip to hold back her laughter.

"Maybe the first tooth is worth five dollars," she said once she regained control. "Losing your first tooth is special. But after that, no. Not from what I've heard at the day care."

"I bet," Dylan said to the children, "you both have beautiful teeth. The tooth fairy will take one look at them, all shiny from being brushed, and think they're special, no matter how many you've lost before."

Tara stared at the blossom of pleased color on her son's cheeks. He'd puffed himself up, nearly beside himself with pride.

In that moment, she knew the future as though a gypsy had foreseen it in a crystal ball. She was going to marry Dylan Ross.

DYLAN TALKED HER INTO STAYING through the morning as they played games with the children. He caught her staring at him, judging him, and it made him nervous. He knew he came up short as a dad. That was the whole point of his proposal.

He talked her into lunch and went about frying bacon for sandwiches. If only he could talk her into being his nanny, but he understood.

"I've been thinking about what you said," Tara started. Her hesitant phrasing prepared him for her refusal. He braced himself, already thinking of counterarguments.

"I can't come up with a better solution," she said. "Not in the time frame we have to work in, anyway. Sure, a grief counselor might eventually help Lily. Might. Eventually. Those words ring hollow when compared with Lily's distress."

Dylan stood agape. Was she accepting his marriage proposal? He didn't doubt she'd say "yes, I'll marry you" by claiming there wasn't a better solution. Thankfully, he wasn't emotionally wrapped up in this woman. She'd be the death of any ego he had.

"An outstanding lawyer," she continued, "which I can't afford, *might* win in court, but I won't risk Jimmy's welfare on 'might.'"

"So you'll marry me?"

Tara sighed with resignation. "Yeah, I guess so."

He didn't know whether to thank her or ask her to go home. If she left, she might come to her senses. "Let's tell the kids."

She grabbed his arm as he turned and a spark of awareness flooded his body. The force of his response surprised him.

"Don't you think we should plan out a few things? Like where we'll live?"

"Sure," he said. "Where do you want to live?"

"My place has a fourth bedroom and a yard. Lily hasn't really settled into your place, so I don't see the point of uprooting Jimmy."

The comment about Lily didn't sit well with Dylan, but he couldn't deny the truth of her statement. "Fine. Anything else?"

"You'll sleep in the fourth bedroom. We can set it up as an office for you for appearances, but we'll also put a sofa bed in there." She bit her lip. "Is that all right? Because sleeping together is a deal breaker."

A guy's pride could only take so many hits. "What makes you think I'd want anything different?"

Her shoulders relaxed. "All right then. But you can't be dating or you know…" She waved her hand. "Be seen with another woman. It would indicate our marriage isn't all it should be, which might damage my case."

"Don't worry, Tara. I can go without sex for a couple of months."

He'd probably work himself to death trying to keep his mind otherwise occupied, but he could do it. "Anything else before we tell the kids?"

"Tons, but nothing urgent. There's no time like the present."

The children came at her call and the four of them settled around Dylan's table again. He glanced at the boy, hoping this worked out well for him, too. The enormity of the changes in all four lives made Dylan hesitate. Was he being *too* selfish?

"Kids, we have good news," Tara said.

Lily and Jimmy glanced up at her then Dylan. He smiled but let Tara take the lead. This would affect Jimmy the most. The boy would have to share his mom, whereas Lily would welcome the change wholeheartedly.

"Lily's dad has offered me a kind of a job," Tara said, "but I'll still work at the Wee Care, and you'll both still go to day care there."

Jimmy continued looking at her, unblinking.

She took a deep breath. Dylan held his. So much depended on Jimmy's reaction to her next words. The kids looked curious, not alarmed. Dylan guessed the tension in the room was his own nerves. Would this work? Was it crazy? He knew one of those answers.

Tara broke eye contact with him and looked at her son.

"Mr. Ross and Lily are going to move into our house for a while. I'm going to help him out since he doesn't have a wife."

"Doing what?" Jimmy asked.

"You'll live with me?" Lily whispered.

Tara glanced at Dylan for help.

"Miss Tara will be with us as long as we need her," he told Lily. "As for what she'll do, well, she'll take care of all of us."

"Brush my hair?" Lily pulled a strand forward.

He smiled at his daughter. "Yes."

"Lily, listen." Tara stroked the hair from the girl's face. "Don't expect always, okay? I'll be with you for a couple of months. At least until you start kindergarten. Maybe a little longer. We'll see. Okay?"

Lily frowned. "Just for the summer?"

"Yes, for the summer, for sure. But we aren't going to tell anyone that because it might change. Then people will just get confused and there would be a lot of explaining. It would get complicated."

"It's nobody's business but ours," Dylan put in. "We'll be a family while we live with Miss Tara and Jimmy, but we can't stay there forever."

Tara looked at Jimmy. "What do you say, honey? It'll be like a long sleepover."

Dylan held his breath. Not that they'd let a child decide this, but the boy's agreement would make it easier.

Jimmy looked at him and then Tara and finally shrugged. "'Kay."

"But," Dylan emphasized, "we're keeping this plan to ourselves. Just the four of us. Everyone else might think it's forever, and that's okay. We let them think that."

Lily nodded. "I can keep a secret. Mommy taught me."

I'll just bet she did. Dylan smoothed the scowl from his mind in case it showed on his face. "Good. Jimmy, you okay with this?"

The boy's chest puffed out. "I can keep a secret, too."

Dylan smiled. What a great kid. "I'm sure you can. Then we're set?"

Tara shrugged. "I guess so. Oh, and Mr. Ross and I have to go through a ceremony downtown so we can all live together."

"A living-together ceremony?" Lily asked.

Tara blushed at Dylan's low chuckle. Lily's innocent query had them both thinking of sex, he was sure. Not that he needed prompting; these days, it seemed to be all he thought about. Had his future bride lain awake last night as well, imagining them together? A purely male satisfaction welled inside him.

"Yes," Tara said.

Dylan started before he realized she had answered Lily's question, not his unspoken one. She referred to the ceremony that would bind them as husband and wife. He rubbed his chest where the bacon sandwich must have expanded against his sternum. A little burn formed there. He shouldn't eat so fast.

"Do I got to go to it?" Jimmy asked.

"No, if you and Lily want to stay at Lily's aunt and uncle's house, that's fine."

The kids glanced across the table and held a silent conference.

"We'd rather play at Uncle Adam's," Lily said in her whisper voice.

"That would probably be best," Tara said. "This is just boring grown-up stuff."

"What kind of job is it?" Jimmy asked.

"What?"

"You said it's a kind of job."

"Oh." Tara cleared her throat. "I'll take care of Lily, just like I take care of you. Making sure she's ready for school, putting her to bed, seeing that she eats healthy stuff. Like a nanny."

Or a mother. Dylan glanced at Lily. All good so far.

Jimmy made a face. Dylan noticed the order in which she delivered her information, hiding the diciest aspect in the middle. Quite the strategist. He'd be wise to remember that.

"Mom likes healthy stuff." Jimmy shook his head in pity for Lily.

"I'll still be doing all those things for you, too, honey. Nothing is going to change between us." She paused. "Except we'll all live together. So you two can play together whenever you want."

"You'll keep your own bedroom, sport," Dylan said. "Lily, you can not only bring all your toys, but your own bed."

He waited for the boy's reaction. *Please let him be happy about this.*

Jimmy stared at the tablecloth for several long beats before he spoke. "If we're like a family, is she gonna call you Mom?"

Tara shook her head. "I'm still Miss Tara to her. I'll be like a babysitter, but she'll live with us. That will be less confusing at the Wee Care."

Jimmy's scowl eased but his face showed the gears turning as he thought it over. "I guess it's okay."

Dylan almost slumped to the floor as the tension left his body.

"Lily?" Tara asked.

Lily's exuberant nod of approval sent her hair flying.

"What do I call you?" Jimmy asked, pointing toward Dylan.

Dylan wanted to tell the boy to call him whatever he felt comfortable calling him. But he waited. Obviously he wouldn't be *Dad,* though why that should bother him, he didn't know.

He met Tara's steady gaze, knew she wanted to tell Jimmy to continue to call him Mr. Ross. "Mustn't get too familiar" was written on her face.

"You can call him Dylan," she said, relenting.

Dylan recognized the line in the sand. Her son, her side. And damned if he didn't want to obliterate it and cross over. Their marriage should be a joining together, not a sorting out.

Maybe it was time to clear up a few things with his bride.

Tara watched the kids rush to Lily's room to play. A heavy silence pushed between the newly betrothed couple as they finished the dishes.

"What will you tell your family?" she asked when she could stand it no longer. So many details to work out. So many emotional minefields to dodge. So many sexual vibrations to ignore.

Dylan blew out a breath. "I'd like to tell Adam and Mom, but…if Mom's called in to testify at your hearing as your employer, I don't want her to perjure herself to protect our secret. So, I guess we tell them nothing."

Tara swallowed and draped the dishcloth across the faucet. "Then it's just us committing fraud?"

Dylan turned to her and took her hands. "Look, we're

in it now. I'll do whatever I need to for Lily, but if you're not certain, I have to know."

"We couldn't wait to get married," Tara said, rehearsing the story she would be telling everyone—even under oath. "We're trying to make it work. I don't have to specify what 'it' is."

"That's my girl."

She cocked an eyebrow. "Only on paper. And I find it unsettling that your praise comes after I agree to lie in court."

"I know. I'm taking advantage of your feelings for Lily."

"No." She shook her head. "Lily and Jimmy will both benefit. If I didn't believe that, I couldn't go through with this. No way can I let the Summerfields take Jimmy from me."

"Okay then." Dylan pulled her forward and brushed a kiss on her lips.

Despite the thrill of the light kiss, she eyed him with reproach and pulled away, tucking her hands safely in the pockets of her shorts. "Dylan."

"Just to seal the deal." His playful grin had her wishing, just for an instant, their circumstances were different. The idea of them living together, of her feeling this attracted to him every day and every night, made her tense. A kiss meant nothing more to him than a smile.

"Do you know how to do this?" she asked.

"There's a loaded question if I ever heard one."

She groaned. "You know what I mean. I've never gotten married before."

"Neither have I, but I did research it last night."

The knot in her stomach dissolved like melted butter. "You researched it?"

"Sure." He grinned at her. "The internet is a powerful tool."

She laughed at the reminder. A computer search would be second nature to him, like a potter using his hands to create.

"We have to go together to apply for the license, and then we can get married right away."

"No waiting period?"

He shook his head.

"No blood test?"

Again, a negative shake.

"No certificate of sanity?"

Dylan laughed. "No, and thank heaven for that. For a license, we just need identification and fifty bucks. I can go Tuesday, if you can get time off to run to the courthouse in Independence."

The speed of the process took her breath away, while her prospective groom's matter-of-fact detailing of chores wrenched something inside her. Not that she expected romance, or even wanted it from Dylan. But she'd envisioned her wedding differently. As a love match, for one thing.

"I'm sure my boss will understand." Irony laced her tone.

He grimaced. "I don't like lying to my family, either. It's just the best way to keep everyone else out of trouble."

"This is all such a mess."

"It's the right thing for the kids, though."

"Remembering that will see me through this." She leaned back against the counter.

"Do you have a minister you'd like to have perform the ceremony? We could get married by a judge at the courthouse on a Friday or Saturday, but I think we should steer clear of involving too many court officials."

"I agree, and there's no one in particular. Jimmy and I have been hit-and-miss about attending church. Although this might be a good time to start praying."

"I can see I'm going to have to be the optimistic partner in this marriage. Fortunately, Mom, Adam and Anne attend regularly with the kids, so the family name is in good standing, if not my own." He ran a hand down her arm. "Would it be all right with you to get married in Adam's backyard?"

She ignored the tingle evoked by his caress. The man was a toucher. She'd have to get used to his habit and stem her initial reaction to frequent physical contact. Innocent contact. Meaningless. "That would be lovely. And it will look normal. If it's not too much of an imposition."

"Anne will love it, which is good because we can get married right after we get the license Tuesday."

The blood drained from her face. "This Tuesday? In two days?"

"The sooner the better, don't you think?"

She scrambled for a reason to delay. "But we'll have to move in together afterward. I can't do that on a weekday."

"We can get married Friday, then, and have Mom babysit so no one will know we're not spending our wedding night together. Then we'll move our stuff to your place on Saturday."

"Okay." Things were moving so fast she could barely keep up. When Dylan set his mind to doing something, he considered the details and formulated plans.

"I'll ask Adam to be my witness."

Deep breath, hold, exhale. Getting married couldn't be worse than giving birth, and she'd gotten through that just fine—although she'd had drugs then. "I'll ask Sandy to stand up with me. She teaches at the preschool and has been really nice to me. I'd like to ask your mom, but I hate to drag her into this when…" She shrugged.

"When it's going to end in less than a year."

"When it's not real," she added.

"If Mom knew we were getting married to help Lily adjust and to keep Jimmy, she'd approve."

"If you say so." Tara kept her doubts to herself.

"Should we invite your parents?"

Tara groaned. Could she get an epidural for the wedding as she'd had for the delivery? Being semiconscious sounded better by the moment.

"And the Summerfields, too?" At her scowl, he added, "I know you don't want to see them, but it might help mend bridges. Think how they'll feel when they find out you got married and didn't tell them."

"Do I care how they feel?"

"Perhaps not," he acceded, "but there's no reason to provoke them. They might drop the case if they saw you doing something responsible."

"Marrying someone I've known for less than a month is responsible?"

His smile produced those same tingles his touch did.

"Wait till they see how I charmed you off your feet," he said. "How could you resist?"

"I forgot we have to pretend we're in love. When we're in public, I mean."

His expression sobered. "Oh, right. I'm sure we can do it."

"Lie back and think of England?"

"Don't kid yourself. England would be the furthest thing from your mind." With a chuckle at her outraged squawk, he left the kitchen.

Sexual longing surged through her at the thought of them making love, followed by a stern talk to her libido. *Not now. Not him. Not real.*

Chapter Six

They both asked for Tuesday afternoon off work, planning on leaving the children at day care while they applied for a marriage license. First, however, Dylan, Tara and his mom sat down in her office. He'd go through with the plan no matter what his mom's reaction, but telling her was his and Tara's first test as a couple. His mom's approval mattered to him.

"What's going on?" she asked, glancing at them in turn.

"Remember yesterday how I asked for the afternoon off?" Tara said.

"We've got it covered, don't worry. Why are you here, Dylan?"

"Mom, I've asked Tara to marry me, and she said yes."

His mom dropped onto her chair, head swiveling between the two of them. "You asked...? You said...? You're getting married? But you hardly know each other."

He put his arm around Tara's waist, surprised that her slender form brought out his protective instincts. She so epitomized self-reliance, he sometimes forgot her youth and fragility. Her hair tickled his mouth as he turned to smile at her for his mom's sake.

"What can I say, Mom? You've always said she's perfect

for the day care, and it turns out she's perfect for me, too."

"I know it's impulsive," Tara added.

"I made her an offer she couldn't refuse."

His mom shot him a skeptical look. "And what was that?"

"She gets me as her husband."

His mom shook her head at Tara. "You should have held out for a better offer."

"Hey." Dylan acted affronted, but he was relieved by her joke.

"Well, I get Lily, too," Tara said.

His mom's expression softened. "Oh, well, then. As long as you're both sure?"

"We are. I don't know what I'd do if she'd refused me." Dylan squeezed Tara's waist, prompting her to echo his words.

"It's the right thing for me, too, Betty."

Tara's tone needed work, but his mom seemed appeased. "When are you going to do it? Have you looked at dates?"

Dylan cleared his throat. "We're getting the marriage license today. We'd like to get married Friday evening in Adam's backyard."

"Friday?" his mom all but shrieked.

"I'm not pregnant," Tara blurted out.

He squeezed his eyes shut for a moment. Of course that's what his mom thought. That was what everyone would think.

"Well, that's a relief." His mother speared him with her steel-blue gaze. "You're already starting married life with two children."

"Mom, a pregnancy's not even possible. I know getting

married so soon seems crazy, but I'd appreciate your support." He held his breath while she studied him.

Finally, she sighed. "Well then, congratulations. And good luck. Do you want the children to stay with me tonight?"

Tara shook her head. "We're just getting the license today."

"But," Dylan put in, "if you'd take them Friday night after the wedding, we'd appreciate it."

Tara stepped on his toes out of Betty's sight as she readily agreed.

Was he supposed to turn down a chance to be with his bride, to have a wedding night? That would look suspicious. "Thanks, Mom. That would be just great."

Tara dug her elbow into his ribs. "Yes, great."

THE LICENSE PROCESS at the Independence Courthouse Annex took less than fifteen minutes, once their turn came. Waiting for that turn gave them plenty of time for second, third and fifteenth thoughts, but neither backed out.

"So," he said outside the license office, "that part is over. You still want to do this?"

At Tara's nod of agreement, he let go of the breath he'd been holding. Help for Lily, he reminded himself again. Help for Lily. This piece of paper might restrain him like a roll of duct tape, but it represented freedom from worrying about his little girl. A fair trade-off, in his mind.

Happy couples beamed for cameras held by family and friends in the bright sunshine. Tara had changed into a pink-and-yellow sundress that made her complexion glow. The functional redbrick building behind her only made her appear fresh and young.

"I think I'm already remiss in my husbandly duties."

Tara looked at him quizzically.

"I didn't tell you how pretty you look. Did you buy that just for the wedding?"

"It's part of my princess wardrobe."

He took that to mean she'd had the dress for a long time. It probably cost more than the black suit he'd donned in honor of his bride, since he hated formal wear. She didn't know him well enough to appreciate his gesture. Still, appearances mattered, especially in their situation.

He'd worn this same black suit two weeks prior at Rosemary's funeral. He made a mental note to retrieve his gray suit from the back of his closet for their wedding.

If his bride could wear the same clothes she had worn as a teenager, she must have been an early bloomer with no inhibition about showing her curves, as the neckline revealed her womanly shape.

Curves he wouldn't get to enjoy, other than visually. This marriage thing had better cure their problems, as he'd no doubt suffer some cold showers and a colder bed.

Or in his case, a colder couch.

He wouldn't even have his condo as a retreat once someone leased it. Sweat coated his skin with icy shivers.

"I can't wait to get it over with," Tara said.

He looked at his bride to be, feeling the same reluctance she wore on her face. Great. "Try to smile. We are getting married in three days."

She flashed him a radiant, albeit fake smile and then kissed him with tight-closed lips. "Better?"

"Just great."

GETTING THE MARRIAGE LICENSE had been no problem, Tara thought. But actually walking outside to get married on a warm summer evening seemed impossible.

This wasn't the dream wedding she'd envisioned as a young girl, but it was the right wedding for her now. She didn't mind her pink dress or having only one attendant. She didn't need a church; she had a backyard of friends and new, if temporary, family. Two teachers of the three-year-olds at the day care, who didn't have class on Fridays, had helped Anne and Betty decorate the yard and house with flowers, and had borrowed and set up chairs. The other teachers split up the day so the day-care duties would be covered with both Betty and Tara gone.

Her father wouldn't walk her down the aisle as she hadn't asked him. Him "giving her away" at this stage of her life and with their past history felt hypocritical. Her parents had agreed to attend, however, and were probably sitting out there now, inspecting and criticizing the simple setup. No doubt they were comparing it to the high-society wedding they'd once envisioned for their daughter. She'd wanted to have only the Ross family in attendance and be married in the living room, perhaps by the fireplace. Dylan had countered that the more "normal" ceremony with friends in tow would appear more convincing in court. She drew the line at inviting Jay's parents.

Outside, as the late-afternoon sun warmed the yard, waited Dylan's coworkers and friends, the immediate Ross family, her parents, the teachers from the preschool, plus her next-door neighbors. Tonight, she and Dylan would go to her duplex and sleep in separate beds. Tomorrow, she and the Ross brothers would move Dylan's and Lily's clothes and things to her house.

If she could get through the ceremony.

A knock came on the door frame of the bedroom where she'd changed into her dress. Dylan walked in, and Tara's breath caught. His silver-gray suit and light pink shirt were set off by a gray silk tie and the pink carnation she'd provided. The wedding colors combined with his blond hair and deep tan sent a zing of desire to her core. The gray in his slate-blue eyes was more pronounced, partly by his outfit and partly by his emotions.

"Wow." He stepped in and took her hand, raised it to his lips for an old-fashioned but delightful kiss. Little tingles sped up her arm at the caress and the look of admiration—and desire—in his eyes.

"You look fantastic."

She smiled. "Thank you. I can say the same for you."

Her pink dress had a full skirt with a fitted waist. Thin straps held up the darker pink bodice that matched the pink roses she carried. She'd dreamed of her wedding gown all her life, but realized in that moment, only the look in her groom's eyes mattered. Although this ceremony wasn't based on love, Dylan's desire brought the same thrill to the pit of her stomach as she imagined a real groom's would have.

"Ready?" he asked.

"As I'll ever be." She took his arm, glad to have him by her side as they walked out to face the crowd of well-wishers.

The gathering stood as they walked between the rows of folding chairs toward the weeping willow tree. Someone had pulled aside branches and secured them with ribbons to create an opening, in which stood Dylan's pastor. Tara kept her gaze on the alcove, determined not to veer from her course.

But her gaze strayed to find Jimmy, beaming a grin as large as Lily's as they stood with Adam and Anne's kids and Betty. Traditionally, he should be on her side of the aisle.

She giggled, drawing Dylan's attention. "Traditionally" she wouldn't have a child at her first wedding.

Against her will, her gaze caught her mother's. Stern, unsmiling and dry-eyed, her mom stood by Tara's dad, who looked equally grim. Both wore impeccably turned-out in clothes more expensive than everyone else's in attendance put together. They didn't blend in, and they wouldn't try to.

Dylan's hand covered hers where it rested on his arm. She smiled at him, grateful for his presence. Without him, she might have faltered at the coldness on her parents' faces.

With each word the minister uttered, Tara expected someone to interrupt and declare them impostors. Dylan squeezed her hand in reassurance before he slid a plain silver band on the finger reserved for her wedding ring. When asked if she took this man as her husband, she replied, "I do," and slid his ring on his finger.

The deed was done.

They greeted the congregation from where they stood by the willow tree as husband and wife, Mr. and Mrs., fraud and cohort.

Jimmy ran to her and jumped into her arms. Lily followed, wanting her hug as soon as she set down Jimmy.

Dylan bent and hugged both children at once. "You both behaved nicely during the ceremony. Make sure you get some cake later."

The kids smiled at each other and ran off, distracted.

"You make a beautiful couple," Betty said, hugging Tara. "Finally, another daughter. How'd I get so lucky?"

A boulder of guilt weighed down Tara's stomach. "I'm the lucky one."

Adam laughed. "Let's hope you still think so in ten years."

"Don't scare her off," Dylan said. "We haven't even had our honeymoon yet."

"Yeah, that'll be scary enough," his brother said.

"You two stop it," Betty broke in. "This is a happy occasion and I'll not have you roughhousing."

Anne took Tara's hands as the "boys" argued playfully with their mother. "It'll be nice to have another woman around to help corral those two." She leaned in and lowered her voice. "I admit I was hesitant at first when Dylan told us you were getting married after knowing each other for so short a time, but I can see you're right for him."

"Thank you. I hope we're both good for each other."

"Oh, definitely," Anne said. "If it hadn't been for Adam, I'd have set my eye on Dylan. Many a woman has tried to snag him. But seeing you with Lily puts my mind at rest."

She stepped back then to allow the next well-wishers to have time with the bride. Tara stiffened as her parents approached. She glanced across the yard to where she'd last seen Jimmy and blew out a breath of relief to find him at the picnic table between Brian and Christopher, drinking fruit punch.

"I'm so glad you could come," she said.

Her father brushed his cheek near hers. "Had to see it for myself. Didn't think you were any too fond of marriage."

"It just took the right man," Dylan interjected, "to talk her into it."

Tara smiled at him, appreciative of his timing. He seemed to sense when she needed support. "Mom, Dad, this is Dylan. Honey, these are my parents, Janine and Barry Montgomery."

Her mother extended her hand to Dylan, her glare boring into him. "Nice to meet you, even at this late date."

"Would have been nicer," her father said, "to meet my daughter's husband before he became my daughter's husband."

The men shook hands, sizing up one another. Neither appeared impressed by his assessment. Tara's chin rose, defensively. Who were they to judge Dylan?

"Well," Dylan said, leaning forward confidentially, "she kind of swept me off my feet."

Tara choked on her laughter, recalling his claim that he could convince everyone their marriage was real. "That's not the way I remember it. You swept me off mine."

He hugged her close. "We swept each other. It was fate."

"I believe that." Fate had certainly brought together the two people perfect for their children's needs.

"Yes, well," her father said, "we wish you luck."

Dylan straightened and stared her father down. "Thank you, sir, but we have more than luck on our side. We have each other, and our children, and our family to help us through rough times."

Her parents moved on without comment.

"Could you have been more aggressive?" she chided under her breath.

"I doubt it," he agreed with a tight smile. "Not in public and definitely not at my wedding."

Tara shook her head, wishing he'd used more caution to avoid provoking her father, but she was touched. "You are amazing. Thank you for being so supportive."

He bent to brush his lips against hers, lingering for a moment. "You're more than welcome."

People around them clapped and cheered, and Tara felt

heat rise in her face. Thank goodness the others would mark it down to bridal nerves. Or was that old-fashioned thinking? Everyone here knew she'd had a child. They probably assumed she and Dylan had slept together. Most of them would be watching her waistline until time proved it unnecessary.

They greeted the rest of the attendees as the afternoon waned. They served the cake—a chunk of which was missing—to one another amidst laughter and threats on her part not to make a mess. Glasses raised in toasts to their future happiness, with punch for the kids and champagne for the adults.

Happily ever after? If only. Tara shut the door on those kinds of thoughts. The man had a child who needed her; otherwise, he'd never have proposed this marriage. Nor would she have accepted if she didn't have a similar need to protect her own child. There was no room in their agreement for sex or long-term wishing.

They kissed the children again and took their leave. The silence in the car between them didn't match the torrent of thoughts in her head.

"That went well," Dylan said.

"I'm glad it's over." She winced. "Sorry. Hardly what a groom wants to hear."

"Don't worry. I'm glad it's over, too, although I hesitate to say that to my bride."

"And that's enough of that nonsense. We both know why we got married. Between us, at least, there should be honesty."

"Right."

Neither spoke as they parked and approached her house. He hesitated as she unlocked the door, sliding her a look.

"What?" she asked.

"Should I carry you over the threshold?"

"Honesty between us," she reminded him. "I'm perfectly capable of walking."

"Okay, then." He waved her in ahead of him.

"I guess I'll go change."

"Tara—"

Please don't let him thank me again.

"Mom said she put chicken salad in the fridge when she was by this morning with the flowers. I rented a movie."

She laughed. "Sounds good. Let me get out of this dress."

He smiled. "Sounds real good."

"Behave." But she wore a smile as she retrieved her pajamas. After cleaning up in the bathroom, she found Dylan loading paper plates in the kitchen, wearing shorts and a T-shirt. Sandwiches shared the surface with potato chips, and raw vegetables with dip.

"That looks fantastic. I'm starving."

He nodded. "I haven't eaten since breakfast. Too nervous."

"I didn't either, but I was keyed up about facing my parents. Why did you get cold feet?"

"Well, I had to get married."

"Temporarily," she countered, pouring pop into iced glasses.

"Still. It makes a man pause. Even Adam got nervous at his wedding, and he and Anne had known each other since the fifth grade."

"But our wedding isn't going to tie you down forever."

"We should toast to that." Dylan took a glass and handed one to Tara. "To our wedding. To keeping Jimmy with you and making Lily feel secure."

Smiling, she clinked her glass against his. "I'll drink to that."

He had chosen an action-comedy movie that made them both laugh. Tara curled into the corner of the couch, wishing for knitting or something to take her mind off of Dylan. Although he occupied the other end of the couch, placing him a full three feet away from her, she felt overwhelmed by his presence. She hadn't been alone with a man since telling Jay about her pregnancy.

Glad when the movie ended, she bade Dylan good-night. "I'll see you early tomorrow."

He followed her down the hall. "I might as well get some sleep. Adam will be here at daybreak."

She paused outside her bedroom door, with Dylan across the hall in Jimmy's doorway. The intimacy, the quiet and the unexpected magic of their wedding ceremony worked against her. She could barely ignore the heavy sexual tension pulsing between them. "Thank you for today."

"We both benefit, or at least our kids do, which is the same thing."

"I don't just mean thank you for marrying me to provide the impression of a stable home life for the courtroom, although I do appreciate that. It was more. You were right beside me every time I needed you."

Dylan took the two steps necessary to reach her. His hand cupped her jaw and brought her lips to his. Sweet and gentle, the kiss lingered between two people becoming friends. Eyes on hers, he ran the back of his fingers down her cheek. "You're welcome. Good night, Mrs. Ross."

"So," ADAM SAID to Tara when he showed up to help with the move, "after your first night as man and wife, do you still want to live with this deadbeat?"

She smiled. "I guess I'll keep him."

"You lucked out, man," he said to Dylan, who replied in a tone too low for her to hear.

Just as well, she supposed, as his comment was undoubtedly an insult to Adam's character. She acted as overseer as they moved things into her house. Their house. They treated everything from Lily's room with extra care. Dylan only moved boxes of clothes, his desk, and a convertible sofa bed, hoping to sublet his condo semi-furnished.

About the time they finished moving, Betty and Anne arrived with the children. Obviously nothing happened in the Ross family without the entire family taking part. Tara liked the idea, but the reality might take some getting used to. Now nine children, one baby and two other adults joined her and the Ross brothers. Their place hadn't grown any and quickly felt crowded with fifteen bodies in it.

"That's cool," Jimmy said, walking in.

Tara turned, realizing he'd picked up a new expression hanging out with Chris all day during the move. All in all, he'd taken this major upheaval in his life well.

If only she could calm her own butterflies.

She looked around the room to see what, in particular, Jimmy considered "cool" and discovered Chris holding a lizard. Make that sixteen bodies.

"Christopher Andrew," his mother warned, "do not bring that creature into this house."

"Aw, Mom," he protested, although more to cajole than to argue. In another second, he and his triplet brother Paul pivoted toward the door.

Tara noticed the longing on Caitlyn's face as she watched her brothers leave, but she didn't budge from Lily's side.

Anne shook her head. "Sorry."

"It's fine," Tara said. She wouldn't want Chris to know,

but she hoped a little of his mischievousness rubbed off on Jimmy. He was too serious for a three-year-old. Becoming part of a large family would be a good experience for Jimmy, even though it was only short-term. She wondered how she would fare living with Dylan, having had only herself to rely on and please for so long. Could she get along with another adult making decisions? Would she be able to share responsibilities—or her son?

Some of the children had found chairs, some plopped on the floor. Dylan pulled dining-room chairs around to face the living room, obviously familiar with entertaining this large group in a small area.

"Let's go play in your room," Caitlyn said. Lily nodded, and they walked down the hall hand in hand.

"My room's here, too," Jimmy told Brian and Bethany. "Come see it."

Three more children left, giving the living-room space and peace. The oldest girls, Mary and Jane, sat on the couch with Penny in her carrier at their feet.

"This place won't be big enough for long," Betty said, looking around.

"It's only temporary, Mom. When the condo sublets, we'll have more income to work with." Dylan flashed a grin. "Besides, it's much more spacious when Adam takes his horde home."

"We're not a horde," Mary said.

"Yeah," Jane agreed, although her hesitant glance at Mary betrayed her uncertainty of the word's meaning.

"We're your family," Mary continued, her eyes twinkling at Dylan, "and you just *wish* we could live here all the time, but you're trying to hide it because you know Mom and Dad would miss us if we moved in with you."

Tara blinked. She hadn't heard Mary tease Dylan before. In fact, she'd barely heard the girl speak.

"Ah, Mary mine," Dylan said, slipping into a brogue and slapping a hand over his chest. "You've discovered my wee secret pain."

Mary giggled.

Dylan turned to his brother, clasping his hands together in a plea. "Can't I have them, really and truly, for my own?"

Adam grinned at Anne and swept his arm out indicating the sofa, front door and hallway. "Only if you take all of them."

Dylan's mouth dropped open. Everyone laughed, and he joined in. Obviously this wasn't the usual answer.

"What's funny?" Paul asked from the doorway.

"We're moving in, too," Jane told him with a smile.

"Cool," Chris said.

Tara smirked at Dylan. "Way to go. Now we're going to need a bigger place right away."

Anne laughed. "You'll need a house with a play set soon so you can send them outside to burn off energy. Adam can build you one like ours."

Tara glanced at them, realizing the family assumed she and Dylan would have children together, even if they believed she wasn't pregnant now. Guilt made her chest constrict.

Paul and Chris looked at each other, then their father, who shrugged. "Sorry, boys. Uncle Dylan wants you, and since I couldn't find gypsies to sell you to…"

"Please don't sell me to the gypsies, Dad!" Chris entreated. "Mom, make him sell us to the circus instead."

"It's not in town," she countered with a sad shake of her head.

"Then you're just stuck with us till the circus comes," Paul said.

Adam sighed, and Anne shrugged. "It was worth a try."

Dylan pretended to wipe sweat from his forehead with the back of his hand. He glanced at Tara. "Whew. That was close."

"I'll say." She'd have to work on her sense of comedy to fit in with this family for the next year. Her comeback felt lame, but she hadn't grown up in a family that joked. In fact, she'd never *met* a family with such a lively sense of humor. Even the children had the timing of stand-up comedians.

"Give me a hand, Brian," Dylan said to Paul. "I need to get some things from the car."

"I'm not Brian."

Dylan frowned in mock confusion. "Really? Well, who-ever you are, come help me."

Paul smiled and followed him out. Tara had caught on to Dylan's game of pretending not to know the children, but she still sometimes blanked when searching for a name.

She and Anne put Dylan's bachelor collection of odds and ends beside her dishes. The cupboards had ample space, even if the house did not. The confusion of "hers" and "his" becoming "theirs" made Tara pause. Some things were easy to blend. She hoped the other aspects of their lives meshed as well as the dishes.

Dylan and Paul returned with ice cream bars for every-one.

Tara raised her eyebrows as the kids gathered around to collect theirs. "Those were in the car?"

"No, we chased down the ice cream truck." Dylan and

Paul bumped knuckles in victory. "I don't think he drove by over where I lived. Getting married was a great idea."

Everyone laughed at his absurdity.

They'd gone out for boxes and chased the ice cream truck instead? Yeah, she'd definitely have to keep on her toes. The idea thrilled her. Even though their size might intimidate her, the Ross family was sheer fun.

She'd have to drag Jimmy away when the time came. For that matter, she'd have to force herself to leave. For not only would she annul the marriage, she'd exit the Ross family. Dylan assured her he'd explain to his mom so her job would be secure, but Adam and Anne might be harder to reconcile to the truth. If they could ever be told the truth.

Later that evening, Dylan plopped on the sofa, aching in every muscle, but feeling a sense of accomplishment for a job well done. He blocked out the thought of the obstacles to come. Tipping back a bottle of beer, he concentrated on just being satisfied in the moment.

Tara had both kids in their beds. Jimmy had viewed the night as an adventure, which Dylan knew would wear off. Lily had settled in bed easily for a change. Tara was showering off the long day—and that was as far he would travel with that train of thought. He'd probably go to work Monday having had his first decent night's sleep in a month, despite it being his honeymoon weekend.

Life was good.

Especially when Tara joined him after retrieving a pop from the fridge, her silver hair wet and her yellow terry-cloth robe short. He cleared his throat and forced his gaze away from her legs. *Would not, could not, or damned I am,* he misquoted Christopher's favorite classic book.

She sank onto the couch and tucked her feet under her. He liked how she made herself comfortable with him.

"The move went well," she said.

"Very. Here's to smooth sailing every day." He held his bottle out and smiled when she brushed her can against it, reminiscent of their toast the evening before.

"You do like to tempt fate," she chided.

If he wanted to do that, he'd pull her still damp body into his arms and investigate under that robe. He'd see how her Diet Coke tasted with his Corona. He'd test her willingness to play some adult games.

He'd ruin everything.

So he tamped down those urges, which he figured he'd be doing a lot of for the duration of their marriage. Hopefully, going through the day-to-day sameness of life together with kids would make him less aware of her as a woman.

"Are you sure you don't want to sleep in my bed?"

Dylan choked, spitting beer as he straightened.

"Sorry." Tara grinned. "I meant that we could switch."

"No, I got it. Just took a minute. And yes, I'm sure. I'll be fine on the couch."

She eyed the length of him. His groin tightened. Dammit. That familiarity thing better set in quick before he did something stupid.

"You're pretty long for a fold-out bed. I would fit better."

He groaned inwardly. If he didn't have his mind in the gutter—or more correctly, in her robe—he wouldn't be interpreting her words as sexual come-ons. Her expression radiated innocence. Maybe she didn't think of him that way.

Part of him wanted to prove her wrong. His brain told

him to cool it. "No, I'll be fine. Uh, sounds like you got the kids down."

"I admit, I'm surprised. Although Lily's so excited, I don't think she's asleep yet. I thought Jimmy would be more troubled. He's never had to share me at home." She yawned. "I'm sorry. I hope you sleep well, but if you don't, please let me know. I wouldn't complain about sleeping on the couch. It's just my size."

She wouldn't have any complaints if he were with her. He'd see to her complete satisfaction. "Tara."

She rose, avoiding him, perhaps seeing his thoughts reflected in his eyes or hearing them in his voice. "I'd best get to bed. Sleep."

He stood. "There will be awkward times, while we get used to living together."

"Right." Her sigh sounded like relief. "But we'll get through them if we remember why we're here."

He stepped closer, pleased when she didn't step away. "We're a team. I want to thank you for agreeing to this. I know it'll work out for both of us."

Tara halted him with her palm out, a millimeter from his chest. "Whoa. I know how you tend to thank me. Let's just shake hands."

He laughed. "Shake hands? What is this, an international banking deal?"

"Let's pretend it is."

"Scared of a little thank-you kiss?"

"Not at all." She smirked. "Thank-you kisses are given on the cheek."

"Is that so?" He'd meet her challenge and show her what he could do with a simple kiss. He grasped her shoulders and pulled her closer.

She turned her head to present her cheek.

Dylan swept his lips across it, then glided near her ear, up to her temple, down to her jaw. Her peach-scented skin made his brain fuzzy. He felt her shiver as her skin heated, and he heard her breathing pick up. She stood still under his caress, safe in their agreement. He put a lot of effort into the kiss, only to discover his own breathing coming more rapidly and his heart racing.

Over a kiss on the cheek?

"Dylan." Tara stepped back, tightening the belt on her robe. A dead giveaway to her nervous state.

"Thank you," he said, amused to goad her.

She shook her head at him. "You're welcome. And let's leave it at that."

"I don't know what you mean."

"You can't kiss me if we're going to live together."

He didn't care for the finality of her tone. "Is that an ultimatum?"

"Take it as you like. Those are my conditions."

He watched her march down the hall after setting the rules. As much as it galled him, he had to admit she was right. Kissing her, breathing in her clean scent and feeling the warmth of her damp skin after her shower night after night would be hell on earth.

He settled on the couch, wondering how he'd ever sleep in pajamas. Driven crazy by the scents and images of a desirable, untouchable woman in the house, he doubted he'd sleep at all.

Yet, that night and the next, he had no problem.

He didn't stir as Tara stopped at his doorway Monday morning, frowning with concern over his cramped position. She'd give him a couple of days and then offer to take the pullout bed again. His rumpled hair begged for her fingers to comb through it. His body would be warm, even though he'd kicked off most of the sheet covering him, exposing a long, muscled male form in stiff, new, navy cotton pajamas. The straining buttons tempted her with a tuft of dark chest hair, and the top of his pants showed a smooth, pale hip bone. She took in his bent limbs and tried not to let his sacrifice soften her resolve. Unhappy with the results, or lack thereof, she quietly turned to get the kids out of bed.

"We're really going to school together?" Lily whispered at the dining-room table, munching dry cereal.

At least Tara didn't have to remind her to be quiet. She'd shushed Jimmy several times, until he finally understood the game of "Don't Wake Dylan." Tara had promised him a kiss and a hug if they could get out of the house undetected.

Which they did.

Dylan woke to the smell of maple syrup. *Lily?* He bolted upright, thinking of the stove and fire. *How had she—?* Then he remembered. He checked his general state of dress and declared himself decent, only to find the house empty. Disoriented, he couldn't recall the last time he'd been by himself. Lily had become such a major part of his life, he felt her absence as though he were a lone shipwreck survivor. He found only remnants of the others. Wet washcloths hanging on the towel bar. Rinsed plates, glasses and a bowl in the dishwasher. A drip of syrup and the tab from a box of frozen waffles on the counter.

His family was gone.

Dylan jerked from the thought. *Lily* was gone. As were the other people who lived here, who were *not* his family. He couldn't afford to get attached. He and Tara would be getting an annulment in three to six months.

Crap. He'd hoped enlisting Tara to help Lily would end his problems, not create new ones. If he got involved with anyone, it wouldn't be with his child's "nanny," regardless of the minor detail of their marriage. He not only depended on her, but he couldn't escape after their affair ended. She'd be here every day.

He certainly wouldn't get romantic with a single mother, given that when he thought of Rosemary, it brought the pain she'd caused bubbling up to the surface. But at the moment, he still had these bizarre, unsettling feelings.

"What the hell am I supposed to make of this?" he asked the empty room.

There was no answer.

TARA MET DYLAN at the door that night, a little unnerved to have someone in her home.

"I brought in the mail," Dylan said. "I hope that's okay."

Tara shrugged. "That's fine. I usually leave it on my desk if that works for you."

"Sure." He handed her a pile of envelopes.

In between the bills and donation pleas from charities lay a personal letter. Tara didn't recognize the handwriting and there was no return address.

After slitting it open, she removed a photograph. "Oh, my God."

Dylan peered over her shoulder before she finished speaking. "That's the two of us."

Kissing.

Tara felt frozen. "Where was this taken?"

"Looks like it's outside the courthouse," Dylan said. "Remember? You couldn't keep your hands to yourself."

"Very funny." She did recall the moment. "But no one was with us. Who took this? Who even knew we were there?"

Dylan blew into the envelope. "There's a sliver of paper." He removed it. "It's a note."

Congratulations. We thought you'd appreciate a memento.
                    J. Albert and Marnie Summerfield

Tara's fingers went numb. "Jay's parents. But how did they know we were there? Even your mom didn't know until that morning."

Dylan shot her a look. "My guess is you're being followed. I'd say the Summerfields hired someone to follow you."

She covered her mouth. "This kind of thing doesn't happen in real life. Who gets followed around? We haven't done anything wrong."

"They want to gather evidence for their case. Their investigator must have been trailing you and got lucky that day when we left the day care."

"Lucky? Huh. We're going to have to be careful in public."

"Or..." Dylan pursed his lips, and his eyes narrowed.

"Or what? That calculating gleam in your eye scares me."

"Don't be afraid." He flashed a grin. "I'm on your side, after all."

"Okay, so what are you plotting?"

"What do you say we use this shadow to our advantage?" Dylan took her hand. "Would you like to go out on a date? It's about time we took this relationship public."

Chapter Seven

"Do you think I should call your mom again?" Tara asked two nights later as dinner progressed. Being in the middle of the restaurant—a table Dylan had requested as most visible—in the nicest, second-most-expensive restaurant in town gave her the willies. She'd left behind her life of paparazzi and having every action watched. Extremely rich families held a certain fascination for some people. She'd never understood it and had never considered it anything more than an annoying part of her life as a teenager. Suddenly, it took on a much more sinister aspect.

How could anyone recognize them in the candlelit room? She could barely see the food on her plate.

"I'm sure Mom has everything under control," Dylan replied. "She runs a day care, for Pete's sake."

Tara nodded. She wasn't used to swanky places anymore, and the Allegro was as swanky as Howard got. She almost longed for a drive-through cheeseburger. If toys came with their meals, the patrons of this restaurant would have something more entertaining to do than to stop by and say hello to her and Dylan. The only people she knew in Howard were from the day care, not many of whom could afford to be regular customers here. Dylan had only returned to town in the past few years, though, and quite a few friends of the Ross family stopped by to see him or to congratulate them on their wedding.

A check of her wristwatch declared it already 9:00 p.m. "What if Lily is crying?"

Dylan took her hand, gazing into her eyes like the lover he wasn't. Not with her, at any rate. "Tara, my darling bride, please stop worrying about the children."

She smiled back, trying on a moonstruck expression. "Husband dear, let go of my hand so I don't have to kick you under the table."

He chuckled and released her. Cutting his steak offered a natural cover for his action. Fortunately, the white-clothed tables sat far enough away from one another that conversations could remain private. Many a marriage had been proposed here, which was why Dylan chose it as the most romantic place in town to be seen.

"Who do you think it is?" Tara asked in a low voice. She shot surreptitious glances around the room.

"Who do I think what is?"

"The P.I. following me. Or us. Have you seen anyone taking pictures? I thought there was a flash earlier."

Dylan shook his head. "There could have been. Someone is celebrating an anniversary a couple of tables behind you. Your stalker might be using that event as cover to take pictures of you."

She shuddered. "Don't call him a stalker. He's probably a nice, harmless grandfather making ends meet."

"If that's what you want to believe. We should give him a couple of money shots."

Her eyebrows rose. "Money shots? In my misspent youth, that meant I should flash him. I'm too mature for that now, thank goodness."

"Amen to that. Wait. Are there any pictures left of you doing that?"

"Very funny. And no." She hoped not.

"Darn. Anyway, I meant let's give him something worthwhile for his time. I don't recall a Lovers' Leap, but isn't there still someplace where the kids go to neck?"

"How would I know? And I wouldn't go anyway. The point is to be out in public, not to sneak off alone."

"Then you'll have to put up with this." He rose and extended his hand. "Will you dance with me?"

Her face heated. "Oh, jeez."

Him standing in the middle of the room, hand out, drew gazes their way. Refusing him, as she wanted to, would also garner attention. She hoped her smile disguised her gritted teeth as she placed her hand in his and let him assist her to her feet.

She squeezed his hand, hard, as she leaned closer. Passing the other tables meant she needed to whisper her objection. "I was eating."

"The food will still be there. Tonight—" he spoke against her cheek "—isn't about eating."

"Trust me," she said as she turned into his arms on the cozy tile dance floor, "I'll be returning to the table after this one song. This place is outrageously out of my price range these days, and the food is too delicious to waste."

His arms enfolded her waist and Tara laid her hands against his strong, hard chest.

"Relax," he said into her hair. "You're supposed to be crazy about me."

Tara met his gaze and trailed a fingertip across his chin, just missing the corner of his lips. His eyes darkened.

"No one is that good of an actress."

His smile flashed before his teeth nipped at her

finger, which she snatched away. "Some women would disagree."

He took her hand and brought the offended finger to his lips, then slid it inside his mouth. And sucked.

Tara swallowed.

"Some women," he continued as he folded her hand in his against his heart, "consider me quite the catch."

"Then how lucky I was to catch you."

He blinked in surprise, and she jerked her head toward a couple to her right, who were now close enough to overhear.

"We were both lucky," Dylan said. "Have I thanked you today for marrying me?"

"Not yet."

His head dipped toward hers. "Then I'll thank you twice as thoroughly later."

The deep timbre of his voice suggested intimacy but carried to those nearby. Tara could have sworn the knees of the other woman dancing buckled momentarily. She could empathize. Her own legs threatened to fold, tumbling both her and Dylan to the floor. Her more base nature wanted to take over.

Lust. She wanted to blame the wine. She wanted to blame Dylan's improper expertise. She wanted to blame the romantic atmosphere in the restaurant, or their charade, or the look in his eyes.

Mostly she wanted to take him home and explore his body.

"That sounds delightful," she said. "I'll hold you to it."

A slow burn ignited her insides as his body responded.

"Definitely hold me to it," he agreed. "To it, against it, inside it."

"We have all night," she whispered. "And I want dessert."

"Me, too."

Tara shook her head, unable to stop a smile. Those women he knew were right—he was good at being naughty.

They returned to the table, his hand low enough on her back to be suggestive. And to affect her mental balance, if not her physical. For the rest of the meal, his gaze stayed on hers. He forked a piece of steak into his mouth, closed his lips around the utensil, and slid it out slowly, wickedly, eyes flirting with hers. One of his hands would find hers, hold it, run his fingers across her skin. By the time dessert came, she couldn't remember what she'd ordered. It said something about the talent of the chef that she even tasted the double fudge amaretto cake.

She rose to go home with Dylan and excused her lightheadedness as a sugar rush.

The humidity wrapped them with lazy longing, and being in the dark car alone intensified the intimacy. She didn't know what to say, how to break the spell or whether she wanted to. Perhaps he felt nothing. Maybe he was simply quiet, plotting their next social foray.

Tara peeked at him. Strong hands lazed against the steering wheel. He sprawled in his seat, the picture of ease.

She couldn't believe it. Had his entire amorous male display just been an act?

They walked into the darkened house together. Brushing past him, Tara thought she heard his sharp inhale. Maybe the *entire* thing hadn't been an act. The thought made her smile with both relief and power.

"Mom." Dylan greeted Betty with too much enthusiasm,

though he kept his voice quiet for the kids' sakes. "How did everything go?"

"Fine." Betty picked up the novel she'd brought and stuffed it in her canvas tote bag. "The children get along together very well. Lily went to bed asking for you, Tara, but it didn't take half an hour to get her quieted down. I've had more trouble with Paul."

"Paul?" Tara looked between her husband and mother-in-law. "Isn't he the gentle one?"

"He's the quietest boy," Betty said. "But compared to Christopher or a three-year-old like Brian, that isn't saying much. Still, he sometimes has nightmares, and during those periods, he fights bedtime."

"I had no idea."

"You'll see it next month," Dylan put in. "For some reason, the middle of July and right before Thanksgiving are bad times for him."

Tara shook her head, resting her hand on Dylan's arm as the child wasn't present to comfort. "Poor little guy."

"Mom." Dylan stepped away. "Let me drive you home."

Tara tucked away a smile, hoping he was stirred up by her touch.

Betty frowned. "Don't be silly."

"I'll follow you in my car then."

"No, you will not. I'll be fine." She turned to Tara. "Good night, dear. Put this sweet but overprotective fellow to bed. And keep him there."

Dylan's color deepened. Tara could have laughed aloud at his discomfort. She, on the other hand, thought it a fine idea. Maybe it was the wine, or the romantic atmosphere of the restaurant, or the intimacy of the dance affecting her. But she was pretty sure it was just Dylan.

He closed the door. "She doesn't like to be coddled."

"She's very independent." Tara flicked off the table lamp, leaving the room in near darkness. Only the hall light illuminated the end of the living room.

"I was going to read a while."

"You were," Tara said in mock agreement. "But I have orders to take you to bed."

"*Put* me in bed."

She placed a hand against his chest and walked him backward. "Take you. Put you. Same difference."

Except for her inflection, which gave the words a much different meaning than his mother intended.

He retreated before her, cooperating on his way to his bedroom. At the door, he balked, becoming an immovable object.

"I'm supposed to put you to bed, remember?" she said.

He flicked on the light switch.

"And keep you there." She stretched on tiptoes and pulled his head down to kiss him. He acquiesced, closed mouth. *This was Dylan Ross, the great lover?* She slid her tongue along the seam of his lips, empowered by his groan and encouraged as his mouth opened.

With a nudge, they traversed the small space and sank onto the mattress. His eyes gleamed with purpose, then he shot up a mental guard.

The strength of his resistance made her realize the depth of the need he fought. She leaned nearer, then closed the distance with a soft kiss.

"Tara." He rested his forehead against hers. "Not a good idea."

Her tongue dipped into his mouth, rewarded by a groan. Dylan moved his mouth on hers, taking over the kiss, and taking her heart soaring. He eased her backward and she clung to him, enjoying the strength of his muscled arms and the weight of the broad chest that came down over her.

"The light," she objected.

"Will make this better for me."

His lecherous grin made her laugh. She tried not to think of faded silver stretch marks or any of her body's other flaws.

Her skin tingled, goose bumps of anticipation rising. *Finally.* The night seemed endless. She would show him how much she desired him, and in return she would have the pleasure of his body and the benefit of his wealth of experience.

She pushed those thoughts aside, determined to enjoy making love with Dylan. Tomorrow—or an hour from now—would be soon enough for regrets.

Her fingers worked at the remaining buttons on his shirt, then raced across the hard planes and coarse hairs they revealed. Air whisked over her legs and abdomen as Dylan raised her skirt.

"Are you sure?" His fingers hooked into her panties to remove them without waiting for her answer.

"Very." She wanted to urge him to go faster. The waiting would drive her insane. She slipped off his shirt and tried to unbuckle his belt while he attempted to pull her blouse over her head.

"A little cooperation here," he muttered.

"A little patience."

He chuckled. "Not likely."

She liked his impatience, saw it as a sign of his desire for her. He shifted to draw off his pants, and an excited warmth rushed through her.

He scooted her toward the middle of the bed, his muscles bulging under her hands as he picked her up. With a heave of her own, she thrust back and upward, and Dylan pulled her clothes out of the way. When his gaze ran over her, he murmured only admiring words, and she relaxed, all thoughts of imperfections burned away by his appreciation.

His eyes gleamed molten blue before his mouth covered her breast. Her gut clenched with need even before his tongue flicked over her distended nipple, before his teeth grazed it, making her arch into him, craving more. He tugged and teased with his fingers on her other breast.

She gasped, her fingers laced into his hair, holding him close, encouraging, although he didn't seem to need it. "Dylan."

"You're beautiful." His words came out muffled, but she wasn't paying attention. What could he say that would be better than what he was doing?

Tara caressed his chest and delighted in the power his responding moan of pleasure granted her. How she wanted to pleasure him. She flicked her thumb across his nipple, and he responded in kind with his tongue.

He kissed his way up her body, scorching a path of need, and slid his hands down to caress her core, dallying on the way. She encircled him with her hand, the smooth heat of his erection heightening her anticipation. It had been so long for her, but this wasn't about sex. She wanted to create this connection with Dylan. She didn't know what she felt for him yet, other than need, but this was an act of giving as well as taking for her.

And she fully intended to take pleasure from him.

His words blurred, as passion-induced words do. At this

point, he should know he didn't have to seduce her. She was his for the night.

"The kids," she reminded him after he groaned loudly. Each squeak of the bed and every moan they uttered worried her.

"Oh." Dylan rose on his elbows and grinned down at her. "Sorry. It's my first time since I brought Lily home."

"It's my first time since I brought Jimmy home."

His eyes widened, then he leaned down and brushed his lips against hers.

Now, she thought. If he used those beautiful, usually meaningless love words now, she'd believe him.

"I'm honored."

Tara smiled and pulled him down, burying her face in his neck. She sucked the cord there, distracting him into another moan as he arched into her.

Each caress he offered now drove her higher. He slowed, taking more time to stimulate her. It being their first time— *only time?*—added depth and meaning, discovery and connection. His intimate touches seared her to her heart. When he entered her, she was more than aroused; she was eager to give him a part of herself. His caresses stirred her and made her writhe with pleasure. They kissed, tongues clashing, then traveling wherever they could reach. She drove herself against him, clasping him closer, straining to become part of him.

Tara gasped as she came, holding in her moan of delight. His climax met hers and meshed the two of them into one being, if only for a brief moment.

Too brief, she thought, as she lay cuddled close, sharing his warmth as his hands soothed her down to reality. His kiss on her forehead broke her heart. It was a kiss of thanks, a kiss of after-sex. Full of affection but none of the love she craved at a time like this.

Many long, quiet minutes later, assured by his heavy breathing that he'd fallen asleep, she slipped away to her own bed. If sex had been a mistake—and it would surely have ramifications she refused to think about—at least she'd shared this need with him. Wishing she had the nerve to sleep in his arms and face him with serene composure in the morning, she slid under her blankets, positive she'd never sleep. She wanted to relive those moments in his arms, extend the fantasy a little longer. But he'd worn her out as well, and moments later she drifted off.

She woke to a hand caressing her hip and lips on hers. Snuggling deeper, she enjoyed the extension of her dream. Dream-Dylan's tongue slid into her mouth at the same time real-Dylan's did.

Tara's eyes flew open. "Dylan?"

"You were expecting someone else?" he murmured against her neck.

"What are you doing?"

His laughter nudged his chest against her breasts. She shivered.

"I would hope it was obvious, otherwise I'm doing it all wrong."

"We can't do this. Not again."

"You were supposed to take me to bed and keep me there. I'd hate to tell my mom you didn't follow through."

Tara evaded his mouth. "We can't."

"We just did."

"That was…hormones. Buildup from dinner."

"I'm still built up, honey. Let me show you."

His body, pressed against hers, convinced her of his aroused state.

"It's okay," he said. "We're married."

"But—" She broke off when his tongue dueled with hers. One hand clasped her close, the other drew circles on her breast, plucking need from the depths of her core. "We agreed not to do this. Married without benefits, remember? That was the deal."

Dylan rose above her. "Are you serious?"

She nodded.

"Okay, then." He kissed her nose. Her cheek. She felt his smile against her neck. "This will be the last time."

LATER THAT MORNING, Dylan appeared crisp and ready for work half an hour earlier than usual. Tara had woken early herself and dressed with care. Dressed for him, though she hated to admit it. Wanting him to find her attractive and needing to feel her best in case he'd changed his mind about their lovemaking, she'd found a knee-length khaki twill skirt and purple camp shirt. They were attractive enough for facing her lover the morning-after, but would hold up to a day of toddlers. She laughed at the mixed-up craziness of her current situation. Meeting his eyes made her squirm, but she forced herself to do so, trying to read his expression. An impossible task.

If they were honest, they couldn't get an easy annulment now. Worse, for the first time in her life, she hadn't even considered protection. Either time.

"How're you doing today?" she asked.

"Good." He grabbed a piece of toast with jelly but shot her a smile. "I have to run."

"Dylan."

"I have an appointment today with my attorney. Everything's fine."

Looking into his eyes, she knew it was true. No guilt, no

second thoughts, no reexamination of their no-sex agreement. He didn't seem to suffer any aftereffects of their lovemaking.

Or even remember it, she thought with pique.

"Bye, pumpkin." He kissed the top of Lily's head.

Lily reached out a hand to him, patting his sleeve. "Bye."

He nodded, then kissed Jimmy's head. "Bye, tiger. You kids have a good day at school."

"Bye, Dylan," he said in a quiet voice. "You have a good day, too."

Dylan stopped in front of Tara. "Thanks."

Thanks? Was he kidding? She nodded, determined to hide her pain with nonchalance.

"I'm sorry I have to rush off."

"No problem."

"You know I'm grateful you take care of the kids while I have to work late or go in early, right?" His eyes gleamed.

"Ri-ight," she drew the word out, watching him.

"So you're expecting this." He pulled her close with his hands around her upper arms and kissed her. Rather than evoking the passion of the previous night, it was the most tender, most heart-touching kiss she'd ever received.

Jimmy hooted. "Look, Lily. Your dad is kissing my mom."

Dylan drew away and winked. She wanted to read promise in his gaze but scolded her imagination. Getting her hopes up would prove painful later.

"Mom, someone's at the door."

Tara laughed. So that pounding noise wasn't her heart? "Are you expecting a delivery?" she asked Dylan.

He shook his head, just as a knock sounded again. "Especially not this early."

He crossed the room and swung open the door, blocking her view.

"I'm looking for Tara Montgomery."

She froze, recognizing the voice. Her mouth went dry. "Jay?"

"Hey, babe."

Dylan stepped back, and Jimmy's father, Tara's ex-lover, entered his home. Dylan inspected him, noting the deep tan against his light blue polo shirt and white cargo shorts. Jay's casual outfit was probably designer expensive, not that Dylan knew or cared, but Tara would recognize the quality of his attire. Dylan bristled at the younger man's arrogant swagger as he crossed to Tara, took hold of her arms and kissed her on the mouth.

The kiss appeared identical to the one Dylan had just given her. Had the dip-wad spied on them through the window by the door?

Tara stepped away and wiped the back of her hand across her lips.

Dylan didn't suppress his smile.

"What are you doing here?" she asked.

"I came to see you. And my son."

Dylan ground his teeth. Providing sperm didn't make this jerk Jimmy's father.

Tara's wide eyes met his, but he couldn't interpret the message. She moved to stand behind Jimmy's chair, putting her hands on his shoulders. "Jimmy, remember what I told you about your father? That he lives someplace else?"

Her son nodded.

"Well, this is your father. His name is Jamison, but

he likes to be called Jay so he's not confused with the hardworking bankers in his family."

"You continued family tradition and named him after me?" He had a goofy grin plastered across his face.

"You didn't know your son's name?" Dylan asked pointedly.

Jay pivoted, eyes narrowed, fake smile widening on his mouth. "I don't think we've been introduced." He extended his hand. "Jamison Albert Summerfield, the third."

Dylan raised an eyebrow, unimpressed. Sure, he'd heard of the Summerfields before Tara mentioned them, a powerful family with interests in every industry in the U.S. He turned to check the effect of the man's presence on Jimmy. The boy had a frown on his face, which could mean any number of things.

"And who's this?" Jay pointed at Lily.

She slid off her seat and shrunk against Tara's side. Tara put an arm around her, hugging both children close. "This is Lily Durant."

Jay turned back to Dylan. "Still didn't catch your name."

"Dylan Ross." He walked around the other man, putting himself between Jay and the others.

Jay nodded, following his progress. His eyes traveled over the foursome, stopping on Lily. "Who's her father?"

"I am," Dylan said.

"I see." Jay nodded then studied Jimmy for a moment. "You don't look much like me."

Dylan faked a surprised expression. "Why, you're right. Jim, you're starting to look like me!"

The boy's eyes widened.

"We both have blond hair. We both have blue eyes. If I had a loose tooth, people would think we were twins."

Jimmy giggled.

Jay scowled. "Your mom was crazy about me back when we were younger. Did she ever tell you about me?"

Jimmy shrugged and left his chair to step closer to Dylan.

"Doesn't he talk?" Jay asked.

"Yes, he talks," Tara said with a glare. "What are you doing here?"

Jay flashed a smile.

Toothy, insincere bastard.

"Can't a guy visit his son?" He ran his eyes down Tara's form, lingering with obvious appreciation, and Dylan's hands fisted. "And the mother of his son?"

"This isn't a good time," she said. "We're on our way to day care."

"Then what, after you drop off the kiddos? You have a charity meeting or a tennis lesson or something? I can come along." He closed one eye in a slow wink. "We can get reacquainted."

Dylan glared. He really didn't like this guy's suggestive wit.

"I'm going to work, Jay. You've heard of work, surely?"

He guffawed. "Not in our circles, babe."

"Be that as it may, I don't have time to catch up now."

"That's cool. I'll just take little Jay Junior here for a ride."

"No," Tara and Dylan said at the same time. She looked at him, but he didn't understand what she wanted him to do. He'd be more than willing to toss the jerk out on his... butt.

"He's not Jamison Junior," Tara added, "or even number four. He's James Alexander, after my grandfather, which you'd know if you read the birth certificate."

"I did, babe. It's just been a while, you know?"

She crossed her arms. "I'm well aware of how long it's been."

The acid in her words made Dylan grin.

"He's not going anywhere alone with you," she continued.

"You wouldn't try to block me from seeing my son, now would you?" His words poured out like rattlers from a burlap sack, slithery and full of threat.

Tara stared him down. "Knock off the games. I'm not impressed."

Jay barked with laughter. Lily put her hands over her ears.

"You never were too easily impressed, were you?"

She must have been at one time. Dylan couldn't imagine the woman he'd come to know falling for this jerk's line.

Tara turned to Dylan. "Can you take the kids to school on the way to your appointment? I'll call and explain the delay."

"Sure, if that's what you want." *Wouldn't you rather I knock him unconscious and throw him in the Dumpster?*

She nodded. "Thanks."

"You heard the lady." Dylan put on his own fake smile for the kids' benefit. "Let's get moving."

"Just leave your plates," Tara said. She gave each child a hug.

Jimmy circled a wide path behind Dylan to avoid the sperm donor. Dylan laid a hand on the boy's shoulder in reassurance, then started when Lily's small palm slid into his hand. He smiled as she held his gaze.

Tara waited until the door closed behind Dylan, which took less time than she needed to pull herself together. Since letting Jay in the house, Dylan had restrained himself, given the way his hands had clenched and his jaw had remained hard throughout their encounter. If only she could mirror his self-control.

Jay looked much the same as always, impeccably groomed, tanned and sophisticated. He'd spent time somewhere sunny, judging by the blond highlights in his hair, which he prided himself on achieving only on the beach.

His charm didn't appeal to her now nor could he convince her of his sincerity. He'd barely spared a glance for Jimmy, other than to assess whether his son shared his own good looks.

She'd been living with a real man this past week. In comparison, Jay was just a very tall boy.

She gathered the children's plates and turned to the kitchen. "What do you really want, Jay?"

He spread his hands innocently. "Just what I said. To get to know my son and to see you again."

"Uh-huh." From past experience, she knew he'd have an angle. "And?"

"And what, babe? Isn't it enough I wanted to visit you?"

She sidestepped as he came closer, keeping the syrupy plates between them. He'd never risk the sticky mess on his clothes. The musky scent of his cologne clogged her throat. Not for the first time, she appreciated Dylan's natural masculine scent.

"Babe, what's the deal here? You sleeping with that guy?"

"That's none of your business." She set the dishes in the sink, wary to turn her back long enough to rinse them properly.

"You've got my kid here while you live in sin?" Jay shook his head in mock dismay. "Corrupting his mind."

"Get off it. Nobody thinks that way anymore, especially you." She couldn't count the number of girls he'd been with before her, and probably a few in the years they'd dated. Taken in by his charm, she'd wanted to believe him when he'd claimed his heart belonged only to her. "Besides, it's not sin. We're married."

Jay stepped back as if she'd slapped him. "You're what?"

She crossed her arms and propped her back against the kitchen counter. "I have to get to work."

"Okay, babe, it's like this." He gave her a shamefaced smile. "I'm in a bit of a fix, and I thought, since I'm the father of your kid, you'd help me out."

Tara gaped at him before she started laughing. Holding her belly with one arm, she wiped at her eyes with her hand. "That's a good one, Jay."

He scowled. "Knock it off, Tara. I'm serious."

That set her off again. The absolute nerve. As though she'd be grateful for his part in getting her pregnant? For what, his expert technique, or his abandoning her once she told him they'd conceived?

"You owe me."

That sobered her like nothing could. She glared at him. "Are you freaking kidding me?"

"All these years, I never bothered you. I let you raise my kid and never threatened to take him away."

Tara went still. "You're on dangerous ground, Jay Three." The pet name irritated him, she could see it in the flaring of his nostrils. "I'll ask one last time. What do you want?"

He thrust his hands into his shorts' pockets. "Money. I'll pay you back."

That would be a first.

"What did you do with yours?" His family pos-
sessed twice the Montgomerys' fortune. "You're not still
gambling?"

"It's not like that."

"Let me guess." She smiled without humor. "It was a
sure thing."

"No, not horses. I learned my lesson there." He dropped
his gaze. "Blackjack."

Casino hopping had been fun, back in the day. The
chances Jay took and the fortunes he wagered added to
the excitement of being with him. Now she could only
shake her head. He had a gambling problem, which might
have started as a relief from boredom but had developed
into a serious addiction.

"What about your trust fund?" she asked. "Didn't you
get access to it when you turned twenty-five?"

He nodded. "It's gone."

Tara dropped onto a chair. "Jay. It's only been two
years."

"I know, I know. I don't need your lectures, too."

"Your family knows?"

He ran a hand through his hair, barely ruffling its expensive perfection. Jay Summerfield might be poorer than
a street beggar, but he'd make sure to look impeccable.

Which she had to admit, he did. But what had attracted
her beyond his looks? He'd introduced her to passion but
also to wild nights at dance clubs and parties with exotic
celebrities. Everyone knew him—probably, she thought
with hindsight, because everyone had loaned him money at
one time. Their relationship had been a spaceship ride, full
of new adventures, exciting risks, and not-so-cheap thrills.
At seventeen, she'd considered him a wild and enthralling
twenty-one-year-old when they'd started dating.

Youth. She could only shake her head and be grateful she'd made it out relatively unscathed.

"I don't have money anymore, Jay. I left home when my parents wanted me to have an abortion." She shrugged. "It was the baby or their fortune. They made it clear I'd have to choose."

Jay opened his mouth but shut it again after catching her eye.

Wise decision.

He swallowed. "I know you don't get control of your trust until you hit twenty-five, but what about your grandmother's money? You got that, right, on your twenty-first birthday?"

He certainly knew a great deal about her financial situation.

"My parents found a loophole in Grandmother's wording, since I left home before I turned twenty-one." She shook her head. "I'd planned on saving that money for Jimmy's college tuition."

"I hear you, T-baby." He hooked an arm under her shoulder, pulling her to her feet and into his embrace. "Not having money is rough."

His definitions of needing money and having it rough probably differed from hers, but she let it go. She stood in his arms for a minute, this alien visitor from the land of Wealth, one of the few people who could understand the magnitude of her loss, but she felt nothing. No thrill of lust or love had survived his defection.

"One kiss," he said, "between friends?"

She shook her head, but he lowered his anyway, claiming her lips in his expert manner, his technique perfected through way too much practice. Once, he'd been like a movie star to her, and she'd been a silly girl blinded by a crush she'd thought was true love.

What she'd shared with Dylan the night before wasn't true love, either. Maybe true love would remain elusive, and maybe someday she'd have to compromise on her standards, but it wouldn't be with Jay.

His forehead creased as he stepped away from her. "You've changed."

"No doubt. It's been more than four years."

"You used to kiss me back. With passion, babe. Don't you remember how hot it was between us?"

"Yeah, Jay, but that's all in the past now. Memories."

Someday, that was all she'd have left of Dylan, too. The air vacated her lungs, making her chest hurt.

DYLAN RUSHED HOME after work—well, after his hours spent at Riley and Ross Electronics, anyway. He couldn't say he'd accomplished much actual work. All day, images of Tara and Jay together had tortured him, although he knew from his mother that Tara had arrived at the day care shortly after he'd dropped off Lily and Jimmy.

It shamed him that he'd called to ask. When the gnawing ache in his gut wouldn't let him concentrate, he'd sought reassurance. Hopefully, Tara wouldn't find out.

Closing the front door, he glanced around his domain. He didn't spot any obvious signs of disruption, but the place felt different. An interloper had invaded his home.

But for now, he only observed Jimmy and Lily in front of the TV set, engrossed in a cartoon of Little Bear. Usually they'd be coloring or playing. Maybe after the morning's upset, Tara had decided to allow them time to veg out. "Hey, guys."

"Hi, Dylan," Jimmy said in a near whisper.

"Hi, Daddy."

Dylan's mouth dropped open. She'd never called him that before. Thinking it better to let it pass, he didn't comment on his new title. Fortunately, Lily wasn't expecting him to as she continued watching Little Bear pick berries. He doubted he could have gotten words past the tightness of his chest anyway. He cleared his throat and suppressed the sappy grin that wanted to explode. "Where's your mom, Jimmy?"

"Getting dressed up." The boy scowled at the TV.

A flaming meteorite crash-landed in Dylan's stomach. "Why?"

Jimmy crossed his arms over his chest, brows lowered and jaw jutting out. "She's going out to dinner with *that guy.*"

Dylan's teeth clenched. "Oh?"

Lily tipped her head back and locked her gaze on his. "Tell her not to go."

"It doesn't work that way, pumpkin."

"Do you want her to go?"

Hell, no. "That's not the point."

His sweet baby grimaced at him, clearly unhappy with his lack of action. He wasn't too thrilled himself.

"Oh, good, you're home," Tara said, coming in the room. A satiny turquoise dress hugged her body and ended way short of her knees. It showed both too much leg and too much chest for her to leave the house. She fastened on a silver necklace with a heart locket and glanced at him. "Dinner's in the oven warming. You can take it out any time you guys get hungry."

He waited for an explanation. Not that she owed him one.

"I'm having drinks with Jay."

"Drinks?" Even he could hear the suspicion in his tone.

She met his eyes. "He spoke to his parents today about their plans." She cut her eyes toward Jimmy. "So I'm going to try to talk him out of siding with them."

"Dammit. That—" He remembered the kids sat close by and caught back the next expletive. "That jerk. Do you think you can convince him?"

Her mouth twisted. "I know what he wants. I'm just not sure I can give it to him."

She'd better not plan to give that loser what he wanted. Dylan clamped his jaw shut, holding his breath as he did when buddy-breathing underwater. *Patience. Trust. And for God's sake, don't panic.* "Is there something I can do to help? Heat some tar and pluck some feathers?" He gave a half grin. "I can enlist Adam and Joe to help me run him out of town."

She shook her head. "Thanks, but no. It's best to deal with him head-on."

"You look nice, by the way. If you can't charm him into seeing sense, no one can."

Tara blushed and brushed at her shiny dress. The turquoise shimmered like the waters of the Caribbean, making her eyes appear darker and larger. He'd like to lose himself in her eyes, watch as they darkened for him as they had when he'd made love to her. Silver hoops adorned her ears. His groin ached as he studied her. His head ached, too, because she'd dressed up for another man.

Dylan tried not to grind his teeth. He wanted to take her down the hall and lock her in her room to keep her from going. Ah, hell, he wanted to lock them both in her bedroom. A replay of the previous night would do them both a world of good. There were things he needed to say. He wasn't positive what they were, but they included, "Don't go out with other guys."

A knock sounded at the door. Tara crossed the room to let in the prince of darkness.

Chapter Eight

Tara stiffened and sensed Dylan close behind her. Her parents stood outside the door. Her mouth went dry. "Mom, Dad. I didn't expect it to be you." She felt an arm go around her waist and the warmth of Dylan's body thawing her chill.

"But we're glad it is," he said. "Come in."

Hadn't he ever seen a horror movie? Once the blood-suckers were invited in, they couldn't be kept out. She gestured them toward the couch, then turned to Jimmy and Lily. "Children, you remember Jimmy's grandma and grandpa from the wedding, don't you?"

They nodded and came over. Jimmy stuck out his hand, such a miniature copy of Dylan, it made her smile.

"And who is this?" her mom asked.

Tara took a breath for calm. Maybe they hadn't met Lily at the wedding. It had been a hectic time and no doubt they'd felt out of place.

"This is my daughter, Lily," Dylan said.

"Oh."

The dismissal in her mother's tone twisted something inside Tara. "Which makes her my stepdaughter."

Dylan shot her a look while she cleared her throat. "You

kids go play down the hall, please, while we grown-ups talk."

Lily tugged on Jimmy's hand and got him to follow her.

Tara blew out a quiet breath, easing onto the love seat beside Dylan. Hopefully Lily hadn't picked up on her comment. Not that it was untrue—she was the girl's stepmother, and felt decidedly wicked, to boot. "Why are you here?"

"Jay Summerfield came to see us today," her father said.

Dylan's hand tightened on hers, the only sign she hadn't gone completely numb.

"He threatened to side with his parents," her mom said. "His approval would make them winning a sure thing."

Dylan's arm moved to Tara's shoulders and he pulled her closer. "We'll fight them every step of the way."

Her dad nodded. "We hoped as much."

"What?" Her pounding heart must have masked his words. She couldn't possibly have heard him correctly.

"No one threatens our daughter."

Tara couldn't contain one sharp outburst of hysterical laughter. No one but them, apparently. She remembered quite a lot of their threats in the past.

"We're offering you the use of our lawyer," her mom said, "at our expense."

"Thank you, ma'am," Dylan said. "Mr. Montgomery."

"But we want concessions," her mom added.

Her father's hand squeezed her mother's. "She means we'd like to talk about some things. We'd like visiting rights and to have the boy stay overnight sometimes when he's older. And we'd like to finance his college education."

Her mom turned on him, even as Tara's eyes widened in astonishment. "Barry, you're giving them everything."

"Well, withholding everything didn't work out so well for us, did it? Tara has a mind of her own. She probably inherited that from your side of the family."

Tara choked on a laugh.

"And," he continued, "she got grit from my side. She left home, a pregnant teenager, and here she is, with a job, a healthy son who seems happy, and a family."

Tears formed in Tara's eyes. She felt Dylan's agreement in the squeeze of her shoulder.

Her dad eyed her mom. "She doesn't need us. I'd like to try to get her to *want* us."

"We don't need your money, sir," Dylan said. "But we'll consider it for Jimmy's future. And the lawyer would be appreciated."

"Call me Barry, please. I admire your stance, and I'll let the offer stand. College money for Tara's children." He grinned. "Including those she inherits through marriage."

"Dad." She rose and met him halfway, hugging him tight and battling tears. "What changed your mind?"

"Jay's visit," her mother said.

Tara sat beside her and hugged her. Her mom sat stiffly in her arms, obviously slower to forgive and forget. "What happened?"

"He wanted to trade his support in this custody battle for money," her father said. "Jackass thought he could buy his way into our good graces. Thought he'd have known better."

"Because you don't have any?" Tara teased.

Her mom's lips tightened, but her dad barked out a laugh. "No, we have a few. But that bastard got my daughter pregnant, abandoned her, and now he wants to help his parents take the child away from my girl, *unless* he's paid enough money? I don't think so."

"But, Dad." She couldn't believe she was hearing this. "You and Mom are the ones who wanted me to have an abortion, kicked me out when I refused, and then refused any overtures from me."

Her dad had the grace to look abashed. Her mother gave her a long stare. "Are you going to hold that against us forever?"

Tara could see genuine fear in the back of her mother's eyes. She and Dylan held all the cards now. The power made her giddy for three full seconds.

"No."

Her mom hugged her close, for the first time since Tara was about twelve. Being rocked in her mother's embrace felt like a long-overdue homecoming.

"Sir. Barry," Dylan corrected.

The two men she...cared a lot for shook hands.

Dylan grinned. "It's nice to meet someone who shares my opinion of Jay Summerfield."

They all smiled, in perfect accord. She wished she could preserve this moment forever.

"So we could arrange to have some visitation rights?" her mom asked.

Tara shook her head. "Grandparents don't need formal visitation rights. Just call and we'll get together. Actually—" She shot a look at Dylan but knew he'd concur. "We haven't made any firm plans yet, but Jimmy's birthday is right around the corner. You should come to his party."

"Great idea," Dylan said. "Tara will fill you in on the details, once we decide on a date and place. In the meantime, the party for Lily's fifth birthday is Saturday at two. We're having it at my brother's house where the wedding took place. You may not have realized it at the time, but most of the people there were my family."

"His brother and his wife have eight children." Tara almost laughed out loud as her parents exchanged a glance.

Her mom pursed her lips. "We thought perhaps your mother had brought all the children from her day care."

"Or you'd rented them from the circus," her dad added.

She and Dylan shared an amused glance.

"I'll tell the boys you said that," Dylan said. "They'll take it as a compliment."

"Let me check my calendar about Saturday," her dad said. "I think I have something scheduled, but we'd like to come."

"Are you planning on a big family, too?" her mom asked.

Tara bumped back to Earth. She wouldn't be having any children with Dylan, unless they'd already conceived a baby. They'd agreed this morning was the last time.

He looked at her, then smiled softly. "We haven't made any plans for babies yet."

"They don't always wait to be planned," her mother said, then covered her mouth, eyes stricken with remorse. "I didn't mean that as a dig, Tara."

"I know, Mom." She couldn't help but think about making love with Dylan the night before and early that morning. Neither time had they used birth control. Was that a Freudian slip on her part—did she want a baby?

Good grief, no. Not now, not in the middle of a custody battle for her son, while consoling her grief-ridden temporary stepdaughter, and married to a man who didn't love her. The very idea caused more hysterical laughter to bubble in her throat. This would be the worst time to get pregnant.

Dylan brought the children back in, and Tara watched her parents play with them for a few minutes. She'd despaired of ever reuniting with her folks, of ever sharing the miracle of Jimmy's existence with them. The sight warmed her heart.

When it registered that Jimmy was whispering to Lily, Tara frowned. Was this a new game? She didn't much like it.

Lily inched over and crawled onto her lap, taking Tara's face between her hands. "Are you really my stepmother?"

Tara nodded, holding her breath.

Lily's tilted her head in consideration. "But you're not wicked. Is that 'cause you don't have no girls like Cinderella's stepmother had?"

"No." She rubbed her nose against Lily's. "It's because I love you and would never be mean to you."

"Thought so." Lily gave her a loud smooch and scrambled back down. "Can we have ice cream?"

Tara narrowed her eyes. Was her claim of niceness being tested? The angelic smile on Lily's face reminded her of Caitlyn and Christopher.

Which made her laugh with genuine amusement.

She couldn't have been happier at that moment. Her estranged parents were in her home, and the children she loved and the sexy man who wanted to be her lover surrounded her. She paused. Okay, if the man felt more than lust for her, she'd be a lot happier, but for the moment, she'd settle for near-bliss. It was enough.

Then the phone rang.

She jerked as though stuck with a pin. Her gaze collided with Dylan's. "I forgot about Jay coming to get me."

"What are you talking about?" her father asked.

"I was going to talk to him about approaching his parents and asking them to back off. I didn't know he'd gone to see you."

The phone rang again.

"We didn't give him anything."

"I know that, Dad. If he offered his parents the same deal, though, siding with them for custody, they'd give him any amount."

"And he'd sign anything for money," her mom said, surprising Tara with her insight into Jay's character. When she was dating him, her parents thought he'd planted the moon with green cheese. No doubt they'd envisioned a Montgomery-Summerfield merger when they married.

Dylan picked up the phone on the fifth ring. "*Ross* residence."

Tara smiled.

"Yes, she's here. Wait, let me check." He moved the phone away from his face. "Honey, did you still plan to meet your old ex-boyfriend tonight?"

Tara shook her head at Dylan. "Behave."

Her dad grinned and caught her arm as she rose. "If you think paying him off would help, we'll loan you the money. We'll *give* you the money."

"Thanks, Dad." She bent to kiss his cheek. "Let me see what he wants first."

"I doubt that's any secret."

Dylan's mouth twisted. "We're in perfect agreement there. Money and Tara."

"And probably in that order," Tara said.

Dylan shook his head. "Clueless about her beauty."

"Always was," her dad said.

"You're the clueless one," her mom corrected. "That girl used her looks like a fisherman uses stink bait."

The men hooted with laughter, making the children stare.

"Gee, thanks, Mom."

Her father handed her a blank check. "Fill in the amount he wants if he agrees to leave town."

"Dad—"

"Or do you want me to go with you to *talk* to him?"

"I was going to offer the same thing," Dylan put in with a wolfish grin.

"Down, boys. I won't be able to negotiate with him at all if you're around."

"You want a woman's touch?" her mom asked. "You never know what two persuasive Montgomery women can accomplish working together."

The men exchanged a glance and groaned as if contemplating a horrific future.

Tara smiled at her mom. "I'd bet we could reduce him to whimpers. Thank you, all of you. But no. I need his cooperation, which means no intimidation. At least not right now."

"You just let us know when," her dad said, his leer resembling the sharklike qualities his financial opponents would recognize.

She took the phone from Dylan and turned her back on the room, feeling their eyes bore into her as she arranged to meet Jay in half an hour. Him waiting in the bar of his hotel wouldn't be a hardship. She only hoped he didn't expect her to pick up his drink tab. The check from her father, should she decide to use it, would be coercion enough. She hoped.

She rushed through tearful goodbyes and hurried her parents along, pausing only long enough for a quick kiss to the children before running out the door.

Dylan glowered but didn't say anything. Being supportive was going to kill him.

THE BIRTHDAY PARTY on Saturday went swimmingly, especially as Adam had opened up their five-foot-deep pool the week before, after the wedding. The Ross men took turns lifeguarding after Adam assessed Jimmy's and Lily's water skills. The two of them hung out in the shallow, three-foot-deep water with the twins. All the kids splashed and screamed while the parents enjoyed cold drinks in the shade. Bright sunshine raised the afternoon temperature into the nineties, and humidity had everyone seeking relief.

Tara's parents dropped in for ten minutes, barely long enough for introductions. "We brought this for Lily."

The birthday girl extended her hand as though she expected to be bitten by a wild dog. "Thank you."

"You're welcome, honey," Tara's mom said. She glanced at Tara. "It's okay if she doesn't open it before we leave. We don't want to put any pressure on her."

Tara frowned as her mom walked over to talk to Betty. Her dad watched Adam at the grill, seemingly interested in the process.

"What's wrong?" Dylan asked at her side.

"Who is this incredibly sensitive woman, and what has she done with Janine Montgomery?"

He swatted her behind, grinning. "What is it you're always telling me? Behave."

Aware of their audience, she winked at him. "Glad you're listening."

Her dad appeared from behind her, with her mother coming a few seconds after. Had her very proper parents witnessed Dylan's playfulness? What would they make of it?

"What came of your meeting with Jay?" her dad asked.

Tara grimaced. "He's being cagey. Said he wanted to 'support' his parents, in the hope of reuniting."

"Humph." Her dad scowled. "You think he's sincere about this heartfelt family reunion, or does he just want to convince them to reverse his disinheritance?"

"Hard to tell. Maybe both."

"He definitely wants money, though," Dylan said. "From somebody."

She nodded.

"Problem is," her dad put in, "a check from me is a finite amount. But access to the Summerfield billions? He'll angle for that if he has any sense."

"Which is up for debate," her mom said.

"Did you try to talk to his mom?" Tara asked.

Janine pursed her lips. "Marnie wants to reconcile with her son. I know how that is, so I didn't push her on the matter."

Tara slid an arm around her mom's waist, still coming to terms with her parents being back in her life.

"Besides," her mom continued, "Marnie does whatever Albert wants."

"So it's wait and see?" her dad said.

"Looks like it," Tara replied.

"Okay, keep us posted. I'm sorry we can't stay."

"We understand, Barry," Dylan said, extending his hand.

The grown-ups said their goodbyes while the children waved from the pool.

Dylan squeezed her waist as they waved goodbye to the retreating car. "I'm glad they came."

She nodded. "If only we could limit all their visits to half an hour or less."

His cell phone vibrated in the clip on his belt and he stepped away to take the call. Tara wondered how long it would take for all of his ex-girlfriends to learn of their marriage. Would knowing stop them from calling? He still visited his condo, she knew, because every once in a while something showed up at her house from there. Not that she suspected him of cheating on her. But Dylan maintaining these ties to his bachelorhood confirmed what she sensed—part of him still longed to be free.

Adam joked with Dylan about which one of them was the real grill master in the family and which should watch the kids in the pool, but his smile never reached his eyes. He darted glances at Anne, sitting in the shade, watching the children.

Betty leaned closer. "She has a headache she can't shake. It's day three."

"Oh, my. Is she prone to migraines?"

The older woman shook her head. "No, which makes Adam worry more."

"Has she seen a doctor?"

"She has an appointment Monday, but she wouldn't hear of us canceling the party. I hope she goes to lie down after we eat."

Tara watched them: the brothers with their easy camaraderie; the children with their own playgroup dynamics; the ailing woman being surreptitiously cared for by all the adults. The Ross family might be wild and crazy at times, but their love provided a strong bond. Tara envied them.

Dylan ribbed his brother while occasionally glancing over at Lily. Not as though he were anxious, but as if every once in a while he remembered to check. Tara couldn't imagine not being alert to her son's movements, but then she'd become a parent when Jimmy had relied on her totally and completely. As a baby, he literally would have died without her care and attention. So she tried to cut Dylan some slack, since he was just now learning to parent. It had only been a few weeks, after all.

Impatient with her judgmental attitude toward Dylan, she scowled at the chicken breast Adam placed on her plate.

"Something wrong?" he asked. He pinched at the chicken with the tongs. "I'll get you a different piece."

She raised her plate up and away, making it impossible for him to remove the chicken. "No, no, it's fine."

"I saw the face you made. It's too charred, isn't it?"

His gray-blue eyes reminded her of Dylan's, except his were slightly darker. The brothers shared the same strong jawline and basic coloring, but Adam came off as more domesticated and less dangerous, even though his construction-worker's body showed more prominent muscle. Dylan still looked like a playboy, an animal more wild than tame.

"It's perfect," she told him. "It wasn't the chicken making me scowl."

Unbidden, her gaze sought out Dylan.

"Ah. If you need me to knock him down for you, I'd be more than happy to."

She gasped in surprise. "What?"

Adam's eyes twinkled. "He's been riding me all day about my cooking. I could use a good reason to take him on."

"No," Betty said, walking up just then. "No arm wrestling—or any other kind of wrestling—today. It's a party."

"Aw, Mom. That's the best time."

Betty swatted his backside. "You two have gotten taller, but I don't think you'll ever grow up." She took Tara's elbow and led her to a folding table laden with bowls of food.

Anne leaned close. "Don't worry, you don't have to eat that chicken. I made barbecued brisket last night."

"Man," Adam complained. "Burn the food one time and they never let you forget it."

Tara smiled at their teasing. As far as she could tell, the chicken looked perfect, although brisket did sound marvelous. Her gaze landed on the dessert, an enormous cake with white frosting and pink flowers. Saliva pooled in her mouth. "That's huge. Who made that?"

Betty's face glowed with pride. "That's my wagon cake."

Tara frowned. Although rectangular, it wasn't decorated as a wagon. "What is it?"

"It's three layers, one each of chocolate, strawberry and white, and we'll have Neapolitan ice cream with it. This way everyone gets a piece with a flavor they like."

"I guess I'm just slow today. Why do you call it a wagon cake?"

Betty laughed. "My late husband used to say the cake was so big we had to have a station wagon to haul it around in, hence the name."

Tara laughed and moved away from temptation, glad for the side dishes. She took bean salad, coleslaw, baby carrots and cut-up vegetables with a spoonful of dip on her plate, along with a little bit of brisket. She left just enough room for a scoop of the potato salad. She hadn't grown up cooking and mastering a dish gave her immense pride.

"You should be able to find something you like," Dylan said, appearing at her side. "You don't have to eat that chicken."

"He threatened to buy fried chicken," Adam called out, "but I told him I'd bar the gate."

"I should have," Dylan shot back. "You burn yours."

"It's not burned. It's just completely cooked."

Tara shut out their voices, amused with their byplay but not interested in the content. She enjoyed watching them interact. This was what a family should be like. The Rosses would present a good model for Jimmy during the time she was married to Dylan.

Jane appeared at her side with a paper plate in hand. "I made the gelatin shapes. Mom did the hot water part, but I cut them out with cookie cutters after she said it was set hard enough."

Tara helped herself to a blue dog and a red flower. "I love gelatin."

Jane pointed to a bowl of multicolored gelatin pieces. "That's the leftovers from around the edges. The boys like those best. Me and the girls like the pretty ones."

Chris popped up on the other side of the table, surprising Tara. He grabbed a wiggly string of gelatin and tossed it in his mouth. "They taste the same."

"Christopher," his mother called. "Use a spoon."

With a grin, he grabbed a spoon and scooped up some more wiggly pieces, then dumped the spoonful into his cupped palm. He slurped the wiggles into his mouth.

"Gross," Jane declared.

"Christopher Andrew," was all Adam said in his deep calm tone. The boy ran off, laughing.

When Betty called for the kids to wash up, Tara's gaze flew to Caitlyn. Fortunately, the girl bypassed the garden hose. She trooped along toward the door behind the others, Lily's hand secured in hers. Dylan met her gaze with laughter.

"Not interested in a shower today?" he asked, coming to straddle the bench beside Tara.

She laughed.

"Dylan Alexander," his mom exclaimed, "what a thing to say to a lady, especially your wife."

She laughed, noting Dylan and Jimmy had the same middle name. The things a woman learned about her husband. "Don't worry, Betty. It's nothing as off-color as it sounded."

"Well, that's a first," she muttered.

When the kids returned, Tara filled a plate for Jimmy, then located him sitting at a table with Brian, Paul and Christopher. *Yikes,* she thought with a smile. Her son was bonding with the second-generation boy terror. Just then, Jimmy grabbed a blue wormlike gelatin piece from Chris's plate, tilted back his head and dropped it into his mouth. Dylan laughed, producing a proud smile on her son's face.

They ate, had cake and opened presents, and the kids jumped back into the pool. Anne went to lie down in her room, needing the dark and the quiet.

Dylan pulled Tara aside for a moment. They stood in the kitchen, watching the family out the sliding glass door.

"What's going on?" she asked. His air of determination while marching her inside gave her a bad feeling. "It's pretty rude to leave the party when your brother and Anne were nice enough to let us throw it here."

"Sneaking away in private is expected of newlyweds. Besides, I want to talk to you about something. And I don't think you're going to like it."

Dread churned her stomach. Due to the chaos surrounding their lives, the possibilities were endless. "What?"

"Did you watch Lily with your parents? Did you see her interacting with my mom? Or when she opened the present Rose's mom sent, how she looked to my mom?"

"Yeah, she seems a little less tentative around your mom now. Maybe her staying overnight with Betty was a good idea."

"I think so, too."

He looked at her as though letting the impact of his words register. Tara didn't get it. So Lily was warming up to Betty. What about that did he think she wouldn't like?

Bile and fear filled her throat. Oh, God, he wanted out of their marriage. He'd only needed her to calm down Lily at night and now Betty would be able to step in to manage that.

She closed her eyes, sick to her stomach. How could he do this, especially after making love to her? She felt exactly like she had when Jay had deserted her four years before.

"Grandparents mean a lot to kids," Dylan said. "The more they have, the richer their lives are."

Tara clamped her teeth together hard, trying to hold on to her composure. *The more they have?* What did this have to do with his leaving—unless she'd gotten that wrong? "You've lost me, Dylan. What are you trying to say?"

"Your parents relented and joined forces with you when you didn't expect them to. They even made an effort to get here today, even though it was out of their way, and it wasn't even for their biological grandchild. They probably didn't really have time, but it was important to you, so they came."

Her stomach uncramped. She didn't understand his objective here, but it didn't seem to have anything to do with him leaving her. "I'm thrilled about that. Their effort didn't escape my notice. But I'm still really confused where you're going with this."

"Just think about it. Maybe being around Jimmy would thaw out Jay's parents."

She jerked away, caught off guard. The situation with the two sets of grandparents were nothing alike. How could he not understand that?

"Dylan, the Summerfields want to *take Jimmy away from me*. Not visit. Not have dinner with him. Not even have him stay for a sleepover. *Take* custody of Jimmy from me."

"You thought your folks were unapproachable and now they're blending in to our family. Or trying to. Maybe if you gave Jay's parents the opportunity, they'd see what a good mother you are and drop the case."

"Forget it. I don't want the Summerfields anywhere around us."

"But—"

"They sicced an investigator on me," she exclaimed, "or are you forgetting that photograph?"

"I'm not forgetting anything, and I'm not saying they aren't committing a terrible, misguided act right now." Dylan inhaled some patience. "They might back down if we gave them some reason to feel included in Jimmy's life."

"No. No, no, no. This isn't up for debate." She slid the

door open, unable to stand and calmly discuss this with Dylan.

"Mom." Jimmy popped up in front of her on the patio, startling her with his quiet voice. "Can we go home?"

Alarm shot through her. She bent and ran her gaze over his face but couldn't detect any illness or distress. Had his quiet voice stemmed from a sore throat?

Dylan knelt beside her.

"What the matter, honey?" she asked. "Are you feeling sick? Is it your throat or your tummy?"

Jimmy shook his head. "I'm tired."

"He's not used to swimming, is he?" Dylan said. "That might have taken it out of you, eh, sport? Or too much cake?"

"I guess."

She didn't like his whispering. He didn't mention a sore ear but an infection might make him lower his voice to decrease the noise level. She wished Anne hadn't had to lie down. Having a former nurse in the family would come in handy, but Tara couldn't ask her to get up and look at Jimmy. He hadn't even complained of any pain.

"Go," Dylan said to Tara.

She glanced from his face to Jimmy to the tables outside in the yard. "But there's so much to clean up. I can't leave it all sitting there."

He stood. "I'll help clean up here. Lily can stay with me so you can take care of the champ here. We'll get a ride home with Mom later."

She hugged Jimmy to her side. "Are you sure?"

"That's the benefit of a two-parent household." He gave her a wicked smile. "Well, one of the benefits."

"Thank you. I know you're unhappy with me about my

decision on the other matter, so it's really sweet of you to be so understanding."

He shook his head. "Tara, just because I don't agree with you doesn't mean I'd want Jimmy to wait around here while you put away food. The boy's sick. Take him home."

She left with Jimmy while Lily was inside with Cait. His daughter barely blinked to find Tara gone. None of the other kids complained of upset stomachs, which reassured him about bad food or a virus. Jimmy would be fine in the morning.

Dylan took shifts cleaning the kitchen while his mom and Adam alternated checking on Anne. Before too long, Adam got shooed back outside and directed the kids in cleaning up the yard while he covered the pool. Everyone had a job, even the little ones who gathered up toys.

Dylan called home to check on Jimmy, who hadn't thrown up but had gone straight to sleep after his bath. He didn't have a fever, which was a huge relief.

When Dylan returned to the kitchen, Adam was tending a pot of spaghetti. Dylan didn't know why his brother would cook again today—there would be leftovers for a week. But sometimes keeping busy took a man's mind off things, so Dylan didn't give his brother a hard time. The poor guy was worried sick about Anne.

Adam picked up Penny from her high chair and rocked away her fretful tears. Dylan could hear the children still playing outside in the half hour left to them before sunset.

"I think Mom's up to something," Dylan said. "A few times I've called her at home and she's been out. When I asked where she'd been, she didn't have an explanation. Said she couldn't remember."

"So?"

"It's like when she planned that trip to Europe without telling us. It makes me wonder what she's up to now."

"What do you think is going on?" Adam asked.

"Do you think she's dating someone?"

Adam rolled his eyes. "Absolutely. That's the obvious answer. Let's shine a light in Mom's eyes until she confesses."

"Don't be an idiot. I'm just saying she's acting suspicious. She was late getting here to help you guys the other week. She never breaks her word, especially about babysitting."

And he and Tara had wound up together. Had his mom been matchmaking? Nah. As she'd barely even mentioned him getting married before he sprang his announcement on her, he discounted that possibility. His mom wasn't built like that.

"So every time someone's acting suspiciously, they're secretly dating?" Adam shook his head. "Man, you've got something on your mind, but I don't think it has anything to do with Mom. It's Tara. Marriage has turned you into a romantic."

"Now you *are* being an ass."

Water boiled out of the spaghetti pot behind Adam, making a bubbly mess. He took a step, stopped, then turned and thrust the baby into Dylan's arms before going to the stove.

"I could get the spaghetti," Dylan said, going into a sway that had become second nature with his nieces and nephews. If only he could bundle Lily in his arms and soothe her this way. Pain pierced him as he thought of all the time he'd missed with her as a baby, time he could never recover.

"You deal with Penny." Adam ran a hand across his jaw.

"She's too young to be teething, but I swear the kid never stops fussing."

Dylan crooned to his red-faced niece, watching his brother from the corner of his eye. Adam had always been unflappable with the other seven babies, even when they'd arrived as triplets and twins. He'd been a model father, who Dylan had planned to emulate someday.

He just hadn't planned to start so soon and definitely not with a toddler who shied from him.

Seeing Adam now, Dylan wondered if his brother had coped well only because he had Anne. Their marriage was a true partnership, based on the love that was driving Adam crazy right now. "You're worried."

Adam tossed a look over his shoulder before cocking the lid on the pot to let steam escape.

"Why don't you let me handle the kids for tonight? Lily's fine here with Cait, and Tara won't mind if I stay over. You could take care of Anne."

"We're fine." Adam dropped into a chair and held his arms out.

"Penny's okay with me." Dylan stepped out of reach. "Honestly, bro, you look like—" he glanced around for little ears "—a bag of you-know-what."

Adam's lips lifted in a humorless smile. "I gave up swearing when Mary started talking. Anne called them 'construction words.' The babysitters were horrified when my sweet baby girl blurted them out like show tunes."

Dylan laughed. "I remember. Mom wasn't too crazy about it either. But seriously, go get some sleep. I'll clean up the kitchen, then stuff the kids in their closets for the night." He glanced down at the snuffling angel in his arms, quieting now. "All but you, Penny-poo. We'll stay up and watch movies."

"No porn."

"So you'll let me help?"

Adam opened his mouth just as a scream sounded outside. Panic clenched Dylan's gut. Lily? He and Adam rushed out to see Jane shaking Bethany, who was lying on the ground near the play set. The other children stood frozen with horror, gazes glued to their little sister.

"What happened?" Adam called, white-faced. "Jane, don't shake her."

Jane jumped to her feet, tears streaming down her face, and tucked her hands behind her back. "Daddy. I didn't do anything. She…she fell off the bar."

Adam squatted next to his three-year-old with Dylan beside him. "I know, honey," Adam said. "It'll be all right."

"I'll get Mom." Paul dashed toward the house.

Jane cried louder, her words incoherent. Dylan pulled her to his side, shifting Penny to a more secure hold to hug the distraught six-year-old. He yearned to push his brother aside, to *do* something, but instinct told him to let Adam handle it. Adam had probably handled hurt children numerous times in his nine years of fatherhood.

"What's wrong?" Dylan asked. "Did she hit her head?"

Adam leaned over his child, ear to her face. "I can't tell if she's breathing."

Several of the kids screamed and began calling for Bethany, their mom and dad, anyone to help.

Adam glanced at the house, obviously looking for Anne. "Call 911."

He could tell his brother was about to panic, and Anne might not even be coherent—Dylan thought she might have taken something for the pain before lying down. He needed to do something.

God, help me.

Letting loose of Jane, he retrieved his cell phone from its holster on his hip. He thrust a now-squirming Penny at Adam, then the phone. "You call."

The children surrounded them now, most stunned into silence at the sight of their sister on the ground, all of them crying. Lily had come over, standing with the girls, tears streaming down her face.

Dylan took a breath to calm himself, then leaned over Bethany and went through the basic ABCs of first aid: airways, breathing and circulation. As he inspected her, following the training he took as a diver, he added in liberal doses of the letter *P:* praying for help.

Establishing her nose and throat were clear, he placed a hand lightly on her chest and leaned down to listen for breathing, hovering near her nose and mouth. No breeze brushed his ear. "I think she just had the breath knocked out of her."

He prayed it was so. Otherwise, he'd have to give her a recovery breath and start CPR. He heard Adam giving his address to the emergency operator. Dylan ran his hands over Bethany's limbs and ribs, checking for breaks, then raised her arms over her head.

Anne rushed out with his mom and Paul trailing behind. "Bethany!"

They were just getting here? Could so little time have passed since Jane's first scream? Fear had stretched the time into hours.

Bethany gasped. Dylan halted his examination as the kids froze around him. Adam caught Anne as she fell to her knees beside Dylan and their daughter.

Bethany gulped and coughed, trying to sit up. Her eyes opened and Dylan's breath whooshed out in relief.

Anne put a hand on her shoulder in restraint. "Stay still, baby."

Adam pushed Dylan out of the way and bent over Bethany to hug her close. "Honey, are you okay?"

Dylan looked around for Penny, relieved to see her fretting on the grass where Adam must have lain her down.

Christopher whooped with joy and jumped around cheering, followed by Paul. Lily and the girls cried harder, smiling and hugging each other, but Brian stood white-faced and frozen, staring at his twin. Dylan folded him to his chest, whispering into his hair. "She'll be okay. She'll be fine. Bethany's okay."

Brian went limp, collapsing in his arms and sobbing. Dylan squeezed his eyes to stem tears of his own. He met Lily's gaze; she didn't look away. When she smiled, he considered it a huge step forward.

Dylan started to laugh, as exuberant as the boys. He'd come through this trial, kept his head and relied on his training, which had, thankfully, leapt vividly to his memory when he needed it. And Lily had smiled at him.

For the first time since bringing his daughter home, Dylan felt optimistic about his future as a parent.

"Thank God everything turned out all right," his mom said later as he sat with her and Adam in the kitchen, sneaking a second piece of cake while the children played in their rooms. "What a chaotic day. Makes my plans seem tame in comparison."

Dylan paused with the root beer bottle to his lips. He shared a bewildered glance with his brother. Hah! he wanted to shout in Adam's face. Which son knew his mother better?

But her tone, as matter-of-fact as if she'd just mentioned the Royals baseball score instead of some mysterious plans of hers, worried him. He did know her, well enough to recognize that her nonchalance masked something he wasn't going to like. "What are you talking about?"

"I'm confident Anne will get a clean bill of health on Monday, so I've rescheduled my trip. I'm leaving for Europe next Friday."

Chapter Nine

Tara had her hands full that week, trying to absorb all Betty had to tell her about running the Wee Care. With preschool classes finished for the summer, she had less to worry about on that front, but more children enrolled in day care. The summer employees had been trained and were working their third week already. The routine was set. Tara just had the pressure of keeping a well-oiled machine running smoothly.

The older woman's announcement had rocked the Ross world.

Tara sat at her own desk for a break, recalling Dylan's arrival home from the party Saturday. After she'd left with Jimmy, Bethany had fallen and Betty had dropped her bombshell.

Her announcement had certainly rocked Dylan, at least. Adam and Anne were handling it fine. Anne's doctor appointment and subsequent testing had revealed unexplained migraines, but at least there was medication to ease her pain until a further diagnosis could be achieved.

Dylan's pain was a different kettle of fish. Plainly put, he'd panicked.

"We'll be fine," he'd said when he told her about Betty's leaving. He sat beside her in the living room, holding her hands. His earnest blue eyes had filled with both trepidation and determination. "We can get through this."

"I'm sure we can." Tara hid her amusement. Good grief, his mother was only leaving for five weeks, not even the three months she'd originally planned.

"Right. Don't worry. I'll be here to help you."

"Thanks." He was the sweetest man sometimes.

"It's just you and me now. We can get through everything if we trust each other. No going off to see Jay without discussing it with me. No relying on Adam and Anne—that would be me who needs reminding about that one," he added with a sheepish smile.

His underlying uncertainty and determination to make everything right made her chest ache with tenderness. He was trying so hard to be a good parent. He'd told her about Lily's response to his helping Bethany.

"She's been looking right at me all night," he said. The awe in his tone acknowledged this as a gift he hadn't expected but had longed for.

If she were ever going to fall in love with Dylan, it would be during a moment like that. When he looked so strong and scared, so brave and uncertain, so capable and needy.

So like a man she could give her heart to. A man she could respect and trust and keep for her own.

But then his cell phone would ring with a call from with one of his "former" girlfriends. While he hadn't met up with any of them, he didn't plan to be married forever.

She'd be wise to keep that in mind.

A WEEK AFTER HIS MOTHER LEFT, Dylan sat on the living-room couch with his laptop, having missed dinner to take part in a phone conference with Joe and a prospective client.

Tara mended clothes at the dining-room table while Lily and Jimmy set up their play area in the living room across from him. He stared into middle space, his mind occupied with a personal conundrum that couldn't be solved, no matter how he manipulated the data.

"Can you play forts with me, Dylan?" Jimmy asked quietly.

"Honey," Tara cut in, "he's working. He can't right now."

Dylan closed his laptop even though Jimmy nodded his acceptance. "I'm not getting anything done at the moment. Just thinking on a puzzle where the pieces don't fit together."

"I like puzzles," Jimmy whispered.

"So do I, usually. This one, not so much. Maybe a break will help me think more clearly."

They built a block wall around Lily, who was brushing her doll's hair to premature baldness. Jimmy guarded her and her baby from dragons, marching his little knight figurine back and forth in front of the wall. Dylan smiled at the kids playing a fairy-tale version of house and went back to the couch.

But his work project appeared as gibberish on his monitor because he couldn't keep his mind clear of the personal. Answers eluded him. Maybe a female perspective would lend him insight.

"Tara." He patted the sofa cushion so they could talk quietly and was grateful when she walked over without his having to explain. "Do you have any idea why a woman would take something that didn't belong to her," he nodded at Lily, "and disappear?"

Tara glanced at the kids engrossed in their play, then

eased down close beside him. "I don't think you'll ever know for sure."

"But why move where she did?" That frustrated him, the not knowing. If only she'd left a diary or written to her mom, but Violet hadn't found anything in Rosemary's belongings so far to give them a clue.

"Maybe you-know-who," Tara said, "wanted to be closer to where you grew up. Maybe she planned to contact you."

"I'm not sure I ever mentioned Howard or even being from Missouri. I think I said the Midwest. I just don't remember." *Does that make me a heel?* He didn't care. Nothing he did while dating Rosemary justified her not telling him about Lily. *That* much he remembered.

"Maybe you should just leave it be then. Try to think the best of her." Tara's eyes beseeched him. "On behalf of all unwed mothers."

Tara's situation was different. She'd told the father of her child. Dylan shrugged, unable to agree to give Rose the benefit of the doubt. What she'd done hurt too much, but if Tara equated herself with Rose, he shouldn't say such things. They didn't need those kinds of recriminations straining their relationship. "I guess I'll never know why Rosemary moved to Salina."

"'Cause it was in Nowhere," Lily piped up from across the room.

Both adults looked at her as she struggled to snap a dress on the doll she'd received for her birthday.

"What did you say, honey?" Dylan asked, his heart pounding.

"Mama said we lived in Nowhere. In the *very* middle."

He cleared his throat. "Lily, do you know why you and your mom lived there? Why she chose that city?"

"So my daddy…" She raised wide eyes to him, her mouth open.

He nodded for her to continue, his gut knotting with dread.

"So you wouldn't find us," she finished slowly. She blinked at him a few times. "'Cause you would take me away from my mama."

He closed his eyes against the raw pain piercing his chest.

"Your mama was wrong," Tara broke in, squeezing his knee. "She made a mistake. Your daddy would have wanted you. He would have wanted to visit and get to know you and take you places, but he would never have taken you away from your mama forever, Lily. Never."

Lily glanced from Tara to Dylan several times, her forehead crinkled, doubt evident in her eyes. "Really?"

"Really," he croaked, not sure if it was true, but it hardly mattered now. Rosemary had made him into the bogeyman. Rage made it nearly impossible to remain seated. He was grateful for Tara's hand on his leg, steadying him. Taking her hand, he held on tightly, glad to have the pressure of her grip to ground him. Leaving the room would make him appear as guilty as he felt. Tara's absolute faith in him not only helped Lily, but it touched him deeply.

He wished he knew for certain that he deserved it.

"Oh." Lily frowned and returned to playing with her doll.

Tara turned to him, but he couldn't let her see his pain. He closed his eyes.

"Dylan," she urged.

"Not yet." *Damn Rosemary to hell! Why would she do that?*

Tara's heart ached. Dylan would never forgive Rose

now, never get over the betrayal. Not able to understand the woman's actions and therefore unable to give Dylan any words of comfort, Tara sat quietly, just being there for him.

No wonder Lily had been so tentative around her daddy. What a hideous thought to put into a little girl's head. That must be why Rosemary hadn't contacted him even when she realized she was ill. She'd backed herself into a corner, unable to call Dylan at that point.

Rose had done a horrible thing. Maybe if she'd been able to face Dylan with the truth, they could have presented a united front for Lily and explained the "misunderstanding." He could have spent the last weeks of Rosemary's life getting to know his daughter and helping out the mother of his child.

Because he would have. Tara knew that with bone-deep certainty. Whatever animosity Rose's actions engendered in him, he'd still have done what was right and best for his little girl. And for the woman who'd given birth to her and raised her.

Because he was an honorable man. The man Tara was falling in love with.

"Violet sent me some letters of Rosemary's," Dylan said hoarsely. "Tidbits of Lily as a baby. Instead of Salina, Kansas, the return address was Middleof, Nowhere, with the Salina zip code. She must have thought that was real damn funny."

"Dylan." Her heart broke at the raw pain and anger in his voice, knowing she couldn't do anything to relieve it.

"I can't be here right now. I'm going to explode."

"Call Adam," she said. "Or Joe Riley."

"Maybe we'll go hit a bar." He rose.

As long as he wasn't alone. Tara ached for him, wishing she had the right to comfort him, or even the words to do so. He must hate Rosemary right now. She feared he wouldn't want her around either.

Some demons a man had to fight on his own.

After putting the kids to bed, with a lot of crying on Lily's part, Tara paced, then tried to read, and wound up watching the clock and listening for the door.

Dylan didn't return until 2:00 a.m., propped up by his business partner.

"He's dead sober, unfortunately," Joe said. "We've been sitting in his old condo, not out in a bar. Do you want me to help put him to bed?"

"I can do it," Dylan muttered, rocking on his heels.

He could barely function. If he wasn't inebriated, he must be emotionally drained. Tara frowned. "Are you sure he's not drunk?"

Dylan snorted.

Joe shook his head. "He hasn't had a drop all night. Said he didn't want to disgrace himself in front of you."

"Shut the hell up, Joe," Dylan said, mild in his exhaustion.

Tara closed her bedroom door behind her, walking Joe out and thanking him. She'd had to put Dylan in her room, for appearances' sake. Alone once more, she wanted to console Dylan while he recovered from this blow. Would he take comfort from her?

When she returned from seeing Joe out, her door stood open and Dylan's was closed. Pausing outside his room, she took a moment to reconsider. Was she doing the right thing? A wiser woman would leave him alone to heal in his own time. A wiser woman would go back to her own bed. But a wiser woman wouldn't have fallen in love with a man who didn't love her.

She tapped softly on his bedroom door. He cracked the door open.

Tara ran her gaze over his haggard face. "I think we should talk."

He stepped back to let her in and sat by her on his pulled-out bed. "I have only one thing to say tonight. I don't think you're anything like Rosemary just because you had a child and didn't marry the guy. I don't want you to worry that Lily's revelation will turn me against you. You are so different. I can't believe I ever thought about you and her in the same breath."

Tara's insides turned to marshmallow. Given his current feelings toward his ex, he couldn't have said anything more moving. "Thank you."

His hand cupped her jaw, eyes looking deep into hers. "You should go to bed."

That's the plan. She moved in closer, their gazes locked. "Shh."

"This isn't a good idea."

She kissed him. "You said that the other night, and it turned out to be an excellent idea."

"I don't want you to feel sorry for me." His lips twisted. "Pity sex."

She put her lips on his and changed the sour expression into desire. "It's not pity."

"If you keep coming to my bed, you can expect the inevitable to happen."

"Okay. So it's inevitable."

"Last chance to change your mind."

Tara waited.

He dove toward her, pushing her back onto the bed. "Thank God you don't listen to me."

That was the last coherent thing she remembered him saying.

THE NEXT MORNING, Dylan had left for work before she woke. His absence had her doubting her action the night before. She shouldn't have gone to his bed. Or, she should have, to comfort him, but not expecting anything to change between them.

"Lily," Jimmy whispered, "do you want to color with me before we got to go to school?"

Tara narrowed her eyes at her son, determined to get to the bottom of this whispering. Tonight, when she put him to bed, they'd have a little heart-to-heart. She didn't think he was mocking Lily—he was way too young to be that cruel, but something was going on, and she'd had enough of it.

Later, Dylan called to say he was working late. Tara tried—and failed—not to read too much into him avoiding her.

She tucked Jimmy in and settled on the edge of his bed. "Honey, what's with all the whispering the past few days? Is it a game?"

He shook his head.

"Then why are you doing it?"

"'Cause of Lily."

Tara frowned, disappointed. Surely she hadn't been wrong? Jimmy was usually so sweet and sensitive. "What about Lily?"

"She's ascared of making noises."

"Why do you think that?"

"She told me so."

She brushed her fingers through his hair, thinking. "Did she tell you why?"

He shook his head again. "Just that she shouldn't. So I figgered I shouldn't either if she's ascared."

Her faith in him restored, she kissed his cheek. "That's sweet of you, honey, but I think we should talk in normal voices. Then Lily will learn she doesn't have anything to be afraid of here."

His face scrunched up as he considered it. "Okay. But not too loud."

"Deal." Tara planted a noisy smooch on his cheek.

"Aw, Mom." He scrubbed at his cheek, his grin showing.

Over the next days, Jimmy alternated between whispering and talking in low tones. Tara never thought she'd yearn for his high-pitched exuberance, but the subdued child didn't act like her son.

Betty noticed it, too, and mentioned his behavior to Tara several days later at the Wee Care. "He's quieted down."

"You'd think that wouldn't worry me, but he doesn't seem like a three-year-old anymore. His entire personality has changed."

"Is he eating and sleeping?"

She nodded. "Soundly. He doesn't even wake up if Lily cries."

"How's she doing with that?"

Tara sighed. "Better. She goes to bed easily enough most nights. I've only had to sit with her twice in the past week."

"That's good, I guess."

She laid a reassuring hand on Betty's arm. "It is. She doesn't act as tentative as she had been."

Betty glanced over at her granddaughter playing with Jimmy. "I'll have to let you be the judge of that."

"Well, at home anyway. I've noticed her studying Dylan more. Making direct eye contact with him."

"That's good. But that means I'm out of ideas about Jimmy."

"He says he's talking quietly because Lily is afraid of loud noises."

"Hmm. That would explain her unease here. It's anything but quiet."

The children laughed and played with clamor. They yelled over each other before remembering their "inside voices." A day care was not a place for soulful meditation.

Tara decided to share the information with Dylan, in hopes he could help Lily feel more at ease. He should know, even though he wouldn't have any more insight into the matter than she did, since neither of them had been around for Lily's early years. It would also give her something to talk about with him other than their night together.

After dinner, she made sure the children had books to look at in Jimmy's room so she could have some time alone with Dylan. Jimmy and Lily decided to "read" their favorites to each other.

She paused outside his door, ignoring the bed pulled out of the sofa. He sat at his desk, shuffling through papers. "Can I talk to you a minute, Dylan?"

He turned. "Please interrupt me. My eyes are crossing. This project is going to make me go blind."

She pulled a chair closer.

Dylan raised his eyebrows. "Not sitting on the bed?"

"It's not that kind of visit. I asked Jimmy about his whispering."

"Is it a problem?"

"No. I thought at first it was a game, then I wondered if he was sick, but that wasn't it. It occurred to me he might be making fun of Lily."

His eyes widened. "Jimmy?"

She shifted guiltily, pleased to hear astonishment in his tone. "It didn't sound like him, but I couldn't figure out another answer."

"Jimmy wouldn't do that, especially not to Lily. They get along great."

"I know."

"Their relationship has been one of the best things about having you two in our lives."

Tara's hands involuntarily clenched into fists, but she quickly reasoned with herself. Just because he didn't specifically mention their lovemaking didn't mean anything. That wasn't the topic under discussion.

Her rationalizing let her set aside her hurt. They weren't supposed to be having sex anyway. Maybe it was better not to talk about it. "Their getting along is why I doubted he'd be mean to her, but you never know."

Dylan shook his head, as though *he* would never have suspected such a thing. "What did you find out? Or did you not come up with an answer?"

"I did. Jimmy says Lily is afraid of making noise."

His brows grew together in a frown. "Did he say why she was afraid?"

"No. I'm not sure if it's something to worry about or something she'll just grow out of as she gets used to being here."

He threw his hands up in a gesture of futility. "She's been like this since I've known her. At first I thought it was losing her mom, the funeral, the newness of everything here, and her grief in general. But she never does really... explode, either with anger or happiness. Even when she suffered constant crying jags, they were never loud."

His phone buzzed, vibrating against the desktop, but he ignored it.

He ran a hand around his neck. "Do you think we should talk to her about it? Or is it better to just leave it alone and see what happens?"

Tara shrugged. "I have no idea, but if we don't address it, we can't help her. Do you think asking her would hurt her in some way?"

"How the hell should I know?" Tilting his head back, he blew out a breath. "Sorry."

"It's okay. I get frustrated, too."

"I'd never have guessed it."

She smiled faintly. "I have a few years more practice."

After a moment, he nodded once and rose. "Okay, let's ask her."

"Now?"

"Why not?"

Tara couldn't think of a reason, so they walked down the hall into Jimmy's room. The children sat on his bed, a book on each lap. Jimmy finished up *Stellaluna*.

"Very good reading," Dylan told him. "Have you read your book yet, pumpkin?"

Lily shook her head.

"I'd love to hear you read," Tara said.

"Okay," the girl whispered. The kids scooted to the middle of the bed, making room for the grown-ups. Tara purposely sat by Jimmy. The more opportunities father and daughter had to bond, the better.

"If You Give a Mouse a Cookie." Lily showed each of

them the cover of the book, mimicking her grandmother/
teacher at school. She whispered her way through the
mouse's adventures, making sure everyone could see the
illustrations on each page. "See?" she said at one point,
glancing toward Dylan with a smile. "He's got powder all
over him."

"He's a funny little guy," Dylan said.

Lily nodded and continued reading.

"Very good," Tara said when she finished.

"Yes," Dylan said. "You're a good reader. You both
are."

He jerked a nod at Tara.

"Let's have some popcorn."

He frowned at her while the kids quietly cheered. As
Tara followed the little ones out of the room, Dylan stopped
her with a hand on her arm.

"I didn't mean get them a treat," he said in her ear. "I
meant for you to ask her about the whispering."

"I know that, but if we ask her now, she might take it as
a criticism of her reading. We need to separate the reading
from the questioning."

He released her arm. "You're right. Again."

She met his eyes, holding his gaze for a moment. His
lack of confidence with his daughter tore at her heart. "I
know only because of my experiences at the day care and
from classes in child development, not some parenting
secret."

"Do you think Lily has a problem? Is that why she reads
so quietly? She's trying to mask it?"

"No. I think Lily is a normal reader for her age. We need
to expose her and Jimmy to other books, though. Expand
their vocabularies and their memories."

"We have plenty." He nodded to Jimmy's shelves.

Tara ducked her head. "Guilty."

"No, it's great. Lily has quite a collection started, too."

"Still, I should take them to the library. We could check out different books and attend other activities for their age group."

Dylan grinned. "At least they know how to be quiet."

Tara smiled and shook her head, preceding him from the room. He could be so wonderful sometimes. Funny and a concerned father. She sighed, none too happy to be drawn to him. Annulment Ahead, she reminded herself. Although the sign would have to read, Danger: Divorce. Their sleeping together negated the possibility of an annulment.

She popped the corn on the stove, letting the kids take turns standing on a stool and shaking the pan. They giggled, the metallic pings and soft thuds of the exploding kernels not bothering either of them.

As they sat in the living room with their bowls, Tara studied Lily. The children sat on the floor while she shared the couch with Dylan. Tara waited for the girl to say something, so she could casually mention the whispering.

"Speaking of noisy things," Dylan started.

Tara shot him a warning look.

"I enjoyed hearing you do the sound effects with your book, Jimmy. It's about birds, right?"

Jimmy nodded then shook his head. "Stellaluna is a bat who gets lost then lives with some birds for a while."

"I like the llama book," Tara said. "Don't you, Lily?"

She shrugged.

After a minute, Dylan asked Tara, "What llama book is that?"

"Well, I have two favorites. *Is Your Mama a Llama?* is really good, but so is *Llama, Llama, Red Pajama*."

He laughed. "I don't think I've heard of that last one, and I thought Adam's kids had every book ever written. Which one do you like better, Jimmy?"

The boy scrunched his nose. "Both of 'em."

Dylan pursed his lips as though considering. "Have you read those stories, Lily?"

She nodded.

He glanced at Tara, lines of frustration bracketing his mouth.

"Which story do you like better, Lily?" Tara tried to phrase the question so she couldn't answer with a nod or a shake of the head but aware Lily might shrug in indecision.

The girl's bottom lip jutted out. "I don't like neither."

"Why not?" Dylan asked.

Tara recalled the stories and almost groaned. Of all the books she'd read to them, why had she brought up those two? She closed her eyes for a moment, dreading Lily's answer.

"'Cause they're about mamas."

Tara couldn't meet Dylan's astonished expression. She felt awful. "I know you like the mouse story, honey. Which other ones do you like me to read to you? Cinderella, right?"

"I like the princesses," she admitted in a grudging whisper. "And Froggy."

Jimmy and Tara laughed. "I forgot about Froggy," she said.

"He's goofy," Jimmy said with admiration in his tone.

"Is this the Froggy who gets dressed, and goes to school, and learns to swim?" Dylan asked.

"Yeah. He's funny." Lily's smile grew. "I like when he gets kissed."

"Eew," Jimmy shrieked before slapping a hand over his mouth, wide eyes turned to Lily. "Sorry."

She ducked her head.

"Why do loud noises bother you, Lil?" Dylan asked.

"I'm not s'posed be loud."

"Why not?"

"It hurt Mama's head."

"Ah." Dylan glanced at Tara and whispered, "Brain tumor."

"Oh," she mouthed without sound. She turned to Lily. "That must have been hard, not making loud noises."

Lily nodded.

"But you know why it hurt your mama, don't you?" Tara ignored the sharp nudge from Dylan's elbow.

Lily glanced toward them but made no reply.

Tara took that to mean she didn't. "Your mama was sick. Her head hurt because something was growing inside that didn't belong there. Her head probably hurt all the time, even when it was quiet in the house. Even when she was alone and no one was making noise."

She waited to see if Lily wanted to add anything about her mom. With an inward prayer that she was doing the right thing, Tara continued, "Your mama's headaches didn't have anything to do with you. You didn't cause them. And you couldn't have stopped all her hurting just by being quiet either, honey."

Lily stared at her popcorn bowl.

When the girl remained silent, Tara went on, "But your dad and Jimmy and I aren't sick, so it's okay to talk in a norm—in your inside voice. It won't hurt our heads. Okay?"

Lily nodded, stirring through the kernels.

Jimmy scooted closer and extended his popcorn bowl out to her. "You can have some of mine."

Near to bursting with love for these children, Tara shared a smile with Dylan. Their gazes locked and her face heated. His eyes darkened and he leaned toward her.

"I keep saying this to you, but thank you again." His breath brushed her cheek, his lips near enough to brush hers if he wanted.

Against her better judgment, Tara wanted him to kiss her. She wanted him to make love to her again. She wanted to give real marriage a shot. They got along well enough and had the children's best interests in common. Based on such common ground, surely their growing friendship could cement their marriage.

And the sex was spectacular.

She moved forward just a centimeter to meet his lips with hers, letting the kiss go on for a moment longer than a mere "thank you" warranted.

He smiled at her. "I have work to finish up."

Chapter Ten

A knock at the door Saturday pulled Dylan from his game of Chutes and Ladders with Lily and Jimmy. Tara had gone to the Wee Care to work on some files she didn't want to bring home for fear of losing them.

A man and woman waited outside the door, their stern disapproval deepening when they saw him. Dylan judged them to be in their sixties or seventies. The woman was wire-thin and pale, the lines around her mouth speaking to a longtime smoking habit. Her gaze bounced from him to the man Dylan presumed was her husband. The man had permanent scowl lines etched in his thick skin and small navy blue eyes as hard as marbles.

"We'd like to speak to Tara Montgomery," the man said.

"She isn't here right now. Perhaps I can help you. I'm her husband." Dylan shook off the bizarre images that phrase generated. Ward Cleaver. Ricky Ricardo. Homer Simpson.

"We know who you are."

A smile flirted around Dylan's mouth. Perhaps the man wasn't speaking for his companion. Maybe this was the royal "we."

Then it struck him. Similar beady blue eyes belonged to Jay Summerfield. Were these his parents?

Tara wouldn't like their presence here, but Dylan wondered if he couldn't find a way to bridge the gap between the two sides. His partner, Joe, was more the negotiator at the firm, but he could mediate if necessary.

"Won't you come in?" he said to the couple.

The man stepped over his threshold with his wife the requisite four steps behind. Their gazes shot to Jimmy, who watched from the floor, he and Lily avid observers.

"That's our grandson," the man said. "I'm J. Albert Summerfield. This is my wife, Marnie."

Dylan extended his hand. "Nice to meet you."

"What does she call the boy?" Summerfield asked. "James?"

Dylan dropped his hand back to his side. He shifted closer to Jimmy, not liking the avaricious gleam in Marnie Summerfield's eyes, as though she'd like to swallow the poor kid. "We call him Jimmy."

"Well, Jimmy," Summerfield said in his deep loud voice, "come on over here and say hello to your grandparents."

Jimmy sat rooted, eyes wide and fingers curled into the carpet. His gaze shot to Dylan, who nodded slightly. He tried to recall his mom meeting Lily the first time in her office. If he could make this easier on everyone he would. Too bad his mother wasn't here now. She'd take control, sort everything out, and have everyone getting along like old friends.

Jimmy rose and positioned himself at Dylan's leg.

Dylan placed his hand on the boy's shoulder. "Jimmy, you remember when your father came here the other day? These are your father's parents. Your grandparents."

Jimmy didn't move, his gaze glued to his grandfather's face.

Marnie stepped forward. "I'm your Grandmother

Summerfield. I suppose you should call me Marnie. Everyone does."

Jimmy nodded.

"Doesn't he talk?" Summerfield asked.

Dylan gritted his teeth as the man echoed Jay's whining query. "Yes, he talks. When he has something to say."

"Well, he could start with hello."

Jimmy's little shaking hand lifted toward his grandfather. "Hello."

Summerfield stared, then a huge smile transformed his face. His pudgy body wobbled with a silent laugh. He shook Jimmy's hand solemnly, watching as the boy exchanged the same greeting with his grandmother.

"Well, how about that, Marnie. He's a little businessman already."

Jimmy wiped his palm on his shorts.

"He sure is," she agreed.

Dylan had the impression she'd agree to any opinion her husband expressed. She was clearly of the subservient-wife generation. He gave an inward chuckle. Tara had learned none of that trait from her exposure to their world, and for that he could only be grateful.

Summerfield stuck out his hand toward Dylan, who shook it with good grace, considering he'd been snubbed only moments before.

"Most people call me Albert. At least to my face."

Dylan smiled, surprised to find he liked the man's sense of self-awareness. "I'm glad you came by, Albert. Marnie. I'm just sorry Tara isn't here. I'm sure she'd like to talk to you."

"She might," Albert agreed.

"Since we made the special trip here," Marnie chirped,

"driving all this way, perhaps we could spend some time with our grandson? Maybe take him to lunch?"

Dylan hesitated. He turned Jimmy around and nudged him toward Lily. The boy scurried off to sit on the floor with his back to the sofa, eyes on the adults, and Lily cuddled up to his side.

Dylan shook his head. "I don't think that's a good idea."

Albert's gaze returned from inspecting the small living room. "Why not? Do you doubt we're who we claim to be? I can prove we're the boy's grandparents."

"I don't doubt that, sir. But Tara isn't here to consent to the idea." Not that she would. If she'd been here, she'd have locked her son in her bedroom by now and thrown herself across the door.

"I'd have to respect that," Albert said. "I imagine she's pretty upset with us."

"You imagine correctly." Dylan eyed him, taking his measure. "And not without cause, if you don't mind my saying so."

"I guess that's one opinion." Albert shrugged. "And many would agree with you, I suppose. But we just learned about our grandson. It's hard not to feel some resentment."

Dylan frowned. "What do you mean? Tara said she told your son when she realized she was pregnant."

"That may be."

"We saw her name and picture in the newspaper a few months ago," Marnie said. "The little boy behind her looked so much like our son when he was that age. And we just knew. The timing was right."

"It seemed impossible no one told *us,* the child's grandparents," Summerfield added. "I called her parents, our former friends. It suddenly made sense why they'd barely talked to us in four years. We thought it was because the kids broke up."

"But Janine and Barry were in Napa the week the picture appeared, so we couldn't get an answer from them."

Silence pulsed between them. Dylan's mind reeled. Tara had kept her pregnancy a secret and hidden Jimmy from his grandparents all these years? He didn't have to imagine their pain and confusion when they'd discovered the truth. He'd lived it.

What would he have done if he'd found out about Lily before Rose died? What if she had blocked him from seeing his child, denied him his rights? He'd have taken her to court and fought for his child, at least for visitation rights, if not shared custody. The Summerfields had just as much right to share in Jimmy's growing up as he had to raise Lily.

"So you hired a private investigator." Dylan still couldn't equate the Tara he knew with a woman mean-spirited enough to not tell her child's grandparents. She denied Jimmy the chance to get to know his family.

"Jamison obviously didn't tell us," Marnie said. "I'm so disappointed in him."

"What do you expect?" her husband countered. "He's been a disappointment his entire life."

"Don't say that, Albert. He's still our son."

Albert scowled and turned his back to his wife. "You can understand our feeling upset when we learned the truth."

Dylan nodded. "Upset" barely scratched the surface of the emotions he'd experienced. He recalled his mom's eagerness to meet Lily, despite having eight other grandchildren she loved. How much more intense would the Summerfields' reactions have been, to learn of the existence of their only grandchild? "Are you saying you overreacted with the lawsuit?"

"We certainly weren't rational at the time."

He could appreciate that. Had they reconsidered, now that they'd cooled down? "So you're dropping the case?"

Marnie stared at her husband's bald spot, while Albert's expression turned cagey. "We didn't exactly say that. If we could spend some time with him, take him to lunch today like Marnie wants, maybe we could feel more at ease about the future. About being able to see him every once in a while."

"That's fair, don't you think?" Marnie insisted.

Dylan conceded their point. "Tara wouldn't like it. You need to arrange this when she's here."

Marnie squeaked with disappointment. "But I'm his grandmother. I should have a place in his life."

"We have rights," Albert said. "Whether the court has assigned them yet or not. And they will." He stared hard at Dylan. "We have the best lawyer money can buy. We have a sympathetic judge assigned to our case. I just happen to golf with him twice a month."

Dylan didn't know whether to believe that, and if it were true, Tara's lawyer could probably ask for a different judge. He didn't know the procedure in cases of bias in family court. Maybe the judge was considered infallible while on the bench. But how could any human not take their friends' wishes into account?

"It would be a shame to see things go that far," Albert said.

Dylan looked the couple up and down. Would lunch with Jimmy really change their outlook on the necessity of the custody hearing? Would Jimmy be all right with them?

They'd been determined enough to hire a P.I. How could Dylan anticipate the lengths they might go to?

"He's our only grandson," Marnie pleaded. "You're too young to appreciate that, but family means everything to the Summerfields. That's why we were so angry with Jamison."

Well, crap. They had to play the grandparent card.

"You can imagine the hot water I'd be in if I let you take Jimmy," he said. "He doesn't know you. That would be frightening for him."

Albert nodded, his lips pursed. "I can respect that. But he can't very well get to know us without spending some time with us, can he?"

"I understand your point, sir, but you have to appreciate my dilemma."

"Come to lunch with us then."

"What?"

"It's not what I'd prefer," Albert admitted. "But this first time, we can see our way clear to including you. We're going to the country club. Do you and the boy have something appropriate?"

"I didn't mean you should take me along," Dylan protested, ignoring his remark about their clothing. "His mother needs to sign off on this."

"His mother isn't here. And the court date draws nearer."

Dylan wouldn't be intimidated by veiled threats. He would be influenced by logic, however. Tara couldn't complain if he accompanied Jimmy. "It will take me a few minutes to get the children dressed." He indicated Lily seated by Jimmy. Thus far, she'd been invisible to the Summerfields.

"That would be fine," Albert said.

"Thank you," Marnie all but gushed.

Dylan found a simple green school dress for Lily and sent her into the bathroom to wash her face and brush her teeth. He found a pair of twill khaki pants in the back of Jimmy's closet, probably leftover from the previous winter. Since Dylan didn't know if the country club would allow shorts, he helped Jimmy into the slacks, ignoring that they hung too short, while Jimmy pulled on a short-sleeved button-down shirt in royal blue.

Jimmy scrunched up his nose. "I don't want to wear this."

"It's all I can find that will look right where we're going."

"Can't I stay home? Kim can come watch me if you gotta take Lily."

Dylan smiled. "Those people are your grandma and grandpa. Just like Miss Betty is Lily's grandma. You want to get to know them, right?"

"Do I gotta?"

"For now, the answer is yes."

Jimmy sighed, a theatrical expulsion he'd no doubt learned from one of the Ross kids.

Dylan helped Jimmy through the hygiene portion then left him while he found "appropriate" clothes himself. Chinos and a polo shirt? Or was that too casual? With a sigh of his own, though less theatrical, Dylan donned his light blue button-down and his gray tie. He'd probably worn this tie more in the past month than in the rest of the time he'd owned it.

Lily needed a few tiny buttons fastened on the back of her dress, but she'd already brushed her hair and managed a ponytail on her own. Granted, the ponytail hung more to the left than center, but overall it wasn't a bad job.

They presented themselves in the front room within ten minutes. Albert gave one nod and rose, leading them out to his Cadillac.

The ride to the club was mostly silent. Intent on keeping the children occupied so they didn't misbehave, Dylan scarcely noted them crossing the state line into Kansas.

Tara would have a seizure. Right after she killed him.

Thank heavens he hadn't let the Summerfields take Jimmy alone.

A valet appeared for the vehicle as Albert slowed in front of a gray stone building. Adam would have admired the 1920s art deco structure and architectural integrity of the building, but Dylan could only contemplate what he'd gotten himself into. Tara was going to go ballistic.

He'd left a note: *Gone to lunch.*

Yeah, she'd love that when the truth was revealed.

The fivesome was shown to a table in the back corner. He'd expected the Summerfields to be shown more deference, especially as the restaurant was only half-filled.

"I asked for this table," Albert explained. "The kids can play right along the balcony there where you can see them. I know children hate to sit for long."

This insight surprised Dylan. Not that he hadn't observed it himself and known it to be true. He just hadn't realized Albert or Marnie knew anything about children. "Tara told me her nanny cared for her when her parents took her out."

"She did. As did Jamison and most of their generation. But nowadays children run wild here."

"It was so much quieter when there was an age limit," Marnie added.

"But not as family friendly?" Dylan suggested.

"No," Albert agreed. "You two kids want to play on the patio until the food arrives?"

Lily and Jimmy looked to Dylan for permission. He scanned the flagstone patio and sturdy carved-stone railing enclosing the area right outside the window where he sat. A purple awning provided shade. "I guess that will be all right."

TARA SPED ACROSS the emergency room, out of breath, her heart thundering. It had taken her forty minutes to drive into Kansas and locate the hospital then find parking. All the while, terror built in her chest. She wouldn't be calm again until she saw the extent of the injury. The sharp smell of antiseptic sawed through her lungs as she rushed to the desk.

"I'm Tara Montgomery," she told the desk nurse. "You have my son, Jimmy, or maybe James, Montgomery here. I heard he hurt his arm."

"Yes, ma'am." The woman pawed through a pile of clipboards. "I have his forms right here. I think he's waiting for Doctor Vargas at the moment."

"I need to see him. Now."

"Yes, ma'am. You'll need to sign this form to have him treated. We obtained a preliminary guardian's signature so he could be evaluated. Do you have your insurance information on you? I'll need to make a copy of your card."

"Can't that wait?"

The woman's forehead crinkled as she peered at the paper. "Now this is strange. Payment has already been authorized. I wonder if someone signed the wrong form." She turned to the computer and clicked keys.

Tara held on to her temper by the skin of her teeth. Everyone had a job to do; this woman wasn't to blame for Tara's dread. That honor lay with Dylan. She dug out her wallet and her insurance card and thrust them at the nurse.

"Thank you, ma'am. I'll also need a form of identification with a picture until I get this straightened out. A driver's license will do, or an employee ID, or a—"

"Look," Tara said. "I understand you have procedures to follow. I'll be glad to fill out those forms and whatever needs to be done to get my son treated. But I need to see Jimmy first. I need to see him *now*."

"I understand you're upset, ma'am."

"No, I don't think you do understand. I'll take the clipboard with me and fill out your forms. Just tell me where Jimmy is."

A woman appeared at Tara's side. She wore magenta scrubs and an air of authority. "What's the problem here, Martha?"

"This woman," she indicated Tara, "refuses to fill out the proper forms to get her son treated. I've tried to explain the process, but…"

The woman's shrug was the last straw for Tara. Tears of frustration and anxiety and anger filled her eyes. Tara turned to the newcomer. "I am not refusing treatment for my son. I just want to see him. I need to talk to whoever is treating him to find out what's wrong and what he or she plans to do before I okay any procedures."

"You haven't seen your son since he arrived?"

Tara shook her head. "I was at work. I only just got here."

The woman took her arm. "Come back with me. I didn't realize."

With a glare at the desk nurse, the older woman turned

Tara toward double swinging doors. Her solicitous insistence worried Tara about the extent of Jimmy's injuries.

"I have four children," the woman said. "I'm Clara, by the way. On behalf of St. Cecilia's, let me apologize for your wait and assure you your son is in good hands."

The tightness in Tara's chest eased a little. "Thank you."

Beyond the doors, the examination rooms were quieter and busier. People cried, both children and adults, and not all of them patients. Tara swallowed her panic.

"He's just in here." Clara indicated a wall of curtains to their right. She pulled back an edge and poked her head in. "You have a visitor."

With a flourish like a magician's assistant, Clara slid open the curtain and revealed the room within.

"Jimmy." Tara hurried toward him, taking in his pale face, red eyes and white sling.

"Mommy!" He burst into tears and tried to lift his arms to hug her, jerking back in pain and crying harder.

"Tara." Dylan rose from the chair beside the exam table where he'd been holding Jimmy's uninjured hand. Lily rushed forward and hugged her legs, burying her wet face against her thigh.

"He was climbing on a railing," Dylan said. "It happened in an instant."

"Don't try to lift your arm, honey." She bent and embraced Jimmy carefully, kissing his cheek, inhaling his sweaty scent. She closed her eyes for a brief prayer of thanks. "Are you all right?"

Jimmy shook his head no, and Tara laughed. "That was a silly question, wasn't it?"

Just seeing him brought her relief. It erased the image of him she couldn't help but conjure up, bloody and mangled and calling her name. She brushed a hand over Lily's hair, realizing the girl was sobbing. "It's okay, Lily. Jimmy's going to be okay."

"I was watching him out the window," Dylan said. "One minute, he was talking to Al—"

She narrowed her eyes at him, waiting for him to continue. "Go on. I'm listening."

"He was talking to someone and the next second, he was falling off the far side of the railing. Just about four feet," Dylan rushed on, as though that were reassuring. "But he landed badly."

"Who was beside him? You said he was talking to someone?"

Dylan grimaced. "Albert Summerfield."

Tara gasped. "You've got to be kidding me."

"We were at some country club. They wanted to take Jimmy to lunch, but I wouldn't let them take him off by themselves. So Lily and I went along."

She stared at him for a moment, unable to deal with this revelation on top of everything else. "Don't talk to me."

She turned to Jimmy.

"Tara," Dylan said, "you've got to listen. I didn't let them take him away by himself, which is what they wanted. He was fine just a minute before. Moments, seconds before."

"Just stop talking." She hugged Jimmy and he nestled into the hollow of her collarbone.

"It happened really fast," Dylan went on. "You know how these things happen. You're around kids all the time. They do something simple and get hurt before you can blink."

She straightened and glared at him. "He didn't get hurt until you were watching him. He wouldn't have done 'something simple' today and wound up in the hospital if you'd been more careful with him. I'm not even going to ask what Albert Summerfield was doing within fifty feet of my son."

"Tara, you know I'd never do anything to hurt Jimmy or let anyone else hurt him. I was watching him."

"Watching him fall over a railing, apparently." She turned away and smoothed down Jimmy's hair, trailing her hand down his cheek.

"Albert went to Admissions on his way out to arrange payment for this before they left."

"They? He and Marnie?" She gritted her teeth. "Don't talk to me, Dylan. I really can't deal with any more from you right now."

"I understand. The priority here is Jimmy. We'll discuss this later, all right?"

She wished someone else would appear who could answer her questions. Talking to Dylan—being in the same room with Dylan—made her want to do him bodily damage. "How bad is his arm? Has a doctor seen him?"

"We're waiting for X-rays, then some doctor—Vegas, I think—is going to review them and let us know what needs to be done."

She kissed Jimmy's head and patted Lily again. "What do you mean, you're waiting for X-rays? For the results or to have them taken in the first place?"

"Radiology is backed up. Someone told me ten minutes, but that was about fifteen minutes ago."

She shot him an impatient look. "So you've just been sitting here, hoping they remember to treat Jimmy eventually?"

His nostrils flared. "I can't exactly leave him and Lily to go chasing down the hall looking for someone who can help."

"Well, I can." She'd find Clara and see if she could hurry the process. She eased Lily onto a chair and turned at the curtain. "Try to keep Jimmy from falling off the table, will you?"

A TRANSVERSE INCOMPLETE fracture of the right ulna. In simple words, Jimmy would be in a series of casts for a while but should be fine thereafter.

Tara watched him sleeping, his baseball mitt night-light shadowing his face. Lily had silently cried herself to sleep, which Tara had only realized when she'd checked on her minutes before. Salty trails marked her cheeks and matted her hair. Guilt pinched her. She hated to think she'd overlooked Lily's needs.

They'd stopped for ice cream on the way home, the four of them tucked in her car, as Dylan had no vehicle. Part of her wanted to let him walk home.

Fortunately, he'd stopped trying to talk to her. She didn't care if he felt guilty. He *should* feel guilty. It was only luck that Jimmy had put out his arm to break his fall. He could have banged his head against the ground.

She looked up at a sound at the door. Dylan stood, backlit by the dimmed hallway light.

"Lily's still asleep," he said quietly. "How's Jim doing?"

"Jimmy is fine." *No thanks to you.* She rose and forced herself closer to Dylan. She still wasn't sure she wouldn't pummel him. She wanted to snap his arm bone.

He didn't move from the doorway. "Can I talk to you?"

"Not in here. I don't want to wake the kids."

"Fine. In the front room? Wherever works for you."

She nodded and he backed away, letting her lead. In

the middle of the room, she pivoted, arms crossed protectively, holding her emotions in. She felt like she'd shatter into a million shards of sharp glass if she didn't maintain control.

"I'm sorry," he said. "I'm more sorry than you know that Jimmy got hurt while I was with him."

"But you weren't with him. You were watching him through a window, from another room." Her voice shook with fury and she reined herself in. "It's not even as if you were taking care of Lily and couldn't be with him. You weren't really watching either one of them that closely."

"I was. Tara, I had my eye on them the whole time."

"While you had drinks with Albert and Marnie?"

"Iced tea."

She waved a hand. "Whatever."

"Well, it's not like I was drunk or on my way to it."

"It's not like you were with the children, either."

"I'm sorry. I thought they were safe. I made a mistake."

Tara inhaled sharply and turned her back to him.

"I know it's not enough to say I'm sorry. There aren't words that will fix this or explain how bad I feel about Jimmy."

She shook her head. He had that right.

"I love him, Tara. It kills me to wonder if I could have done something to prevent this."

She heard the pain in his voice and believed him. Maybe he did deserve forgiveness. Maybe the same thing would have happened if he'd been standing two feet from Jimmy and Lily. Maybe it would have happened if she'd been there.

But he'd betrayed her trust.

"I told you I didn't want the Summerfields around

Jimmy. I said it here, when my parents came by. I said it before the wedding. I said it at Lily's party."

She spun to face him, burning with cold blue fire. "Then you disregarded my wishes. You thought you knew better. You thought it was no big deal. But it is a big deal, Dylan. To me."

"I'm sorry. They said they might drop the case."

She raised an eyebrow, skeptical. "Did they? Did they actually say that? Or did Albert hint around at it?"

Dylan's face went pale.

"I know how they work, with their manipulations and half promises. Just because you don't like Jamison doesn't mean all the problems between him and his parents were his fault."

"They weren't ever told about Jimmy. I thought I was doing the right thing. I thought I was helping."

The fire had burned through her. She felt dead inside, filled with lifeless ash. She studied him. "You know? I believe you."

His shoulders fell in obvious relief.

"But it doesn't matter. You betrayed my trust."

"Does it count for nothing that I was trying to help?"

"I'd like you to leave."

"What? Leave?" The Adam's apple moved in his throat as he swallowed hard. "You mean, leave the room? Because I can give you more time. Time to forgive me."

"No, I mean I wish you didn't live here anymore. I just can't figure out how to make that happen without hurting Lily." Tara shrugged. "She's not ready to adjust to something new, even life without you."

His eyes nearly bulged from his head. "What are you talking about?"

"Ideally, you'd go live at that condo you won't sell and

won't sublet, and Lily would stay with me. Like extended babysitting." She frowned. "But for some reason, you're growing on her and I can't separate you."

"That's my child you're talking about. What makes you think I'd let her stay with you?"

"Isn't that the whole purpose of our marriage? To get Lily settled? And I'm the one who can do that, right?"

"I'm not going anywhere without her."

"I know. More's the pity."

Dylan turned on his heel and stalked out the front door.

Tara watched him go, detached from any feeling.

DYLAN SLAMMED his open hand into the wall at his condo. Damn her. She'd become the ice queen, cold and unreachable. He couldn't blame her for being angry. Hell, he was mad at himself, even though he knew he couldn't have prevented Jimmy's fall if he'd been right there beside him.

But he hadn't been. Albert Summerfield had gone out to tell the kids it was time to eat. Albert had been standing two feet from Jimmy when the boy had backed up against the wall, scrambled onto the railing, then fallen.

Dylan looked around his condo, stunned by Tara's attack. He hadn't planned to sell it, but he hadn't gotten around to subletting it, either. He and Joe had come here the night he'd found out Lily thought he was the bogeyman. He'd come here during the day sometimes, on his way home from work, just to sit by himself and listen to the peace.

He sure had quiet now, although peace proved elusive. This place was only four walls and some furniture. Tara's duplex was home.

And if he ever wanted to return there, he'd better do some hard thinking about his priorities.

The "someday" when he was going to settle down and be a dad and husband had arrived.

DYLAN DID SOME FAST MOVING in the next few days. Tara barely talked to him, but he kept his tongue still and his head low. If she didn't notice him, he could finish all the things he had to do before approaching her.

The first major miracle he needed happened without his intervention. Albert and Marnie Summerfield showed up on Tara's doorstep.

"We brought something for Jimmy," Albert said.

Tara swallowed her trepidation and let them in.

"Hi, Grandpa Summerfield," Jimmy said from his spot by the coffee table. He tried to arrange his knights and soldiers left-handed around a cylindrical oatmeal container he imagined as a castle. "Hi, Marnie."

Tara jerked in surprise. Jimmy greeted them as if he'd known them forever or he saw them every day. As if Albert hadn't been partially responsible for Jimmy's fall.

As if he liked him.

What was going on here?

"Hello, Jimmy," Albert said. "That's a fine cast you have."

"Is that a sleeve or a bandage?" Marnie asked.

Jimmy grinned, his still-wobbly tooth hanging lopsided. He raised his right arm with its dark blue cast. "They come in colors now. I got to pick what I wanted. I almost got yellow instead."

"Colors?" Marnie shook her head in amazement, probably not feigned. "What will they think of next?"

Jimmy tilted his head to one side. "I don't know."

"I'm going to talk to your mother for a minute," Albert said. "If we could go someplace?"

Filled with misgiving, she led him to the kitchen where she could still hear Jimmy's voice. "What is it?"

"First, I want to say I'm sorry for my part in Jimmy's fall." Albert swallowed. "He was playing fine, both him and Lily. The patio at that end is made for kids. It's covered from the sun, and has some toys. Beads on wire tables, magnet games. Calm toys."

"I didn't realize it was a play area." Why hadn't Dylan explained? Because of the guilt he felt?

"It's almost an extension of the dining room, except for the window between us. I didn't know he could climb so fast."

"I understand." Words wouldn't change anything, but she could see how remorseful he felt.

"He wasn't scared. He just wanted to play longer," Albert said. "We've talked about it, Marnie and I, and we're dropping the custody case."

A kick to the solar plexus couldn't have dazed Tara more. She stared, waiting for the other shoe to drop.

"We realized we can't keep up with a child of Jimmy's age and energy."

"Thank you." Tara couldn't feel her face. She hoped her words were intelligible.

"If it's not too much to ask, would you consider some partial holiday visits with the two of you? And we could hire a nanny to help us if you'd allow him to come to our home."

"I think we can arrange something."

Tara saw them to the door, unable to believe her luck.

After setting up *Finding Nemo* for the children, she ran to her room and cried tears of relief. Mixed in were tears of sorrow over how she'd treated Dylan.

THAT NIGHT, Dylan answered his phone, his heart racing to see Tara's number on his display.

"Sure, I understand," he told her.

He turned to the kids. "Mom/Miss Tara is going to be about an hour late. She's going to talk to her parents and wants us to eat without her."

He considered whether it was time to teach the children to set the table.

Jimmy fisted his eyes with his good hand, while Lily's tears slipped silently down her face.

"Hey, now." He squatted down and gathered them in a hug. "She's coming back soon. What's with the grumpy faces? Dinner's in the oven, and then I've got a surprise for afterward."

"What?" Jimmy asked.

"Can't tell you." He stood, hoping to distract them.

Lily tugged on his hand. "Tell us, Daddy, tell us."

"Well, just a little hint wouldn't hurt. You can't have crying faces. And that's all I'm saying."

They hurried through the meal and the cleanup afterward.

"Tell us now, Daddy," Lily said. For the first time since he'd known her, his baby spoke in an almost normal tone. Dylan's eyes filled with tears, and he blinked rapidly so the children wouldn't see. He had Tara to thank for this progress. He had her to thank for so many things. A grin entered his mind as he considered how he'd like to show his gratitude. A kiss would only be the start.

"Yeah, Daddy," Jimmy said, "tell us."

Dylan turned his gaze to the precious boy at his other side. *Daddy?* His chest ached with the truth of it, but he doubted Tara would approve. So he showed them his camera instead of commenting or correcting the boy.

"Pictures?" Jimmy asked. "I thought we was going to play a game."

"You thought we *were* going to play. But this will be fun, too. I can make the images appear on the monitor, and we can make them look funny for your mom's birthday."

"Funny?" Lily scrunched up her nose, and Dylan shot a photo of her. He showed them the image on his digital camera.

"Like this?" Jimmy stuck fingers in either side of his mouth and pulled in opposite directions, crossing his eyes. Dylan laughed and shot that, too.

After several goofy shots of each, he had them pose together and smile sweetly. "Okay, you two. I'll finish by the time the big hand gets to the top." He pointed to the analog clock. "Give me fifteen minutes."

They ran down the hall to their rooms, and Dylan loaded his camera onto his hard drive. The pictures flew across the screen. He saved them and clicked open the appropriate program for manipulation. Centering the sweet shot of the kids together, he softened the edges then overlaid different sizes of the goofy pictures around the border.

The soft patter—which was a misnomer if ever he'd heard one—of their feet sounded in the hallway just as time expired.

"Well?" they demanded in unison.

"*Voila.*" He watched their faces. They both started laughing.

"You did it, Daddy!" Lily hugged his arm.

"Now, I'm going to make these my screensaver."

"What's that mean?" Lily asked as Dylan clicked the appropriate keys, impeding his progress in her attempt to see the changes to the screen.

"I hate to repeat myself, but *voila* again." He waved a hand at the monitor where the goofy images rotated around the stationary sweet one.

"That's so cool," Jimmy breathed in awe.

A tremor ran through Dylan. He'd do anything to keep these kids safe and happy. His plan had to work.

By the time Tara returned, he had the kids bathed and in their pajamas, waiting for her to tuck them in. He watched as she gathered the kids in a hug and led them down the hall to their rooms. While she changed clothes, he kissed each child good-night. Why had parenting ever scared him?

"Don't show Mom the thing we did," Jimmy urged in a whisper. "I want to tell her about it, how we made the funny faces and stuff."

"I'll wait."

Dylan paced the living room, hoping she'd come out so they could talk. He'd drag her from her room if need be, since he didn't want to have this discussion where the kids might overhear.

"How'd it go?" He pounced the moment she walked into the room.

"Fine." Tara slid onto the couch, curling herself into a shell. "They wanted to talk about us all going to Germany for Christmas. I told them we needed to stay home and establish traditions for the kids."

He opened his mouth, then changed his mind. She'd be here through the holidays. He couldn't imagine how they would have made it through Christmas without her, and he would have missed Jimmy.

Her decision only made him more certain of his next words, the words he'd waited a long time to say. "I want to ask you a favor. It's big."

A smile touched her lips. "Bigger than marriage?"

"Almost."

"What is it?"

His heart ached, remembering the day not so long ago when she'd have said, "Sure, anything." Hopefully, he could find that woman again. He needed her.

He'd fallen in love with her.

"Come to my room." When he saw the objection form on her lips, he expanded his request. "I have something in my desk to show you."

She followed him down the hall, sitting on the couch he hadn't converted into a bed yet for the night. The bed he wanted to make love to her on.

He cleared his throat. "You remember I had an appointment with my attorney the day your ex showed up?"

She nodded, eyes huge and face tight.

Dylan hesitated. "What's the matter?"

Tara swallowed, hard, her throat tight with dread. Did he want out of the marriage? She'd suspected him of this before, but now he had cause. She'd frozen him out with her unforgiving attitude. It had been panic over Jimmy. And, she'd admit, a remix of Jay's betrayal four years past making her unable to trust a man she cared for. A man she loved.

Now that he knew why Lily had feared him, he could deal with her better on his own. Not that there seemed to be much of a problem left. Lily had started to thaw toward Dylan when he'd helped Bethany after her fall. She'd come to trust him, to the point where she could admit why she'd feared him in the first place.

She rose. "I'd like to sign those papers, Dylan, but I can't."

His forehead creased in a frown. "Why not? Wait a minute. What do you think this is?"

She couldn't look at him and wished she could flee, but pride held her still. "Our annulment papers."

"What makes you think I'm leaving you?"

His remark arrowed in on her most basic fear like a rifle scope magnifying a trophy buck.

"I'm not going to run off to Portugal, Tara."

Her face went cold. She realized she'd been holding on to her fear of abandonment all this time. Not dating. Not totally trusting Dylan. Holding up her parents' rejection and Jay's desertion as the behavior to expect from anyone who claimed to love her.

His silence drew her gaze.

"Don't you think it's a little soon for an annulment?" he asked. "You promised to stay until Lily was settled in kindergarten. Five minutes ago, you said you'd stay through the holidays."

"I can't sign them anyway."

He stepped closer and tipped up her chin, the warmth of his fingers burning her skin. Or was that guilt?

"Why not?"

"Because we had sex. We can't get an annulment now."

Dylan's hand fell away. "Is that the only reason you won't sign them?"

She shook her head.

His grin took away her breath. Blue-gray light shone from his eyes, confusing her. "What's the other reason?"

"We didn't use protection."

He stepped back.

"I never should have come to your room," she rushed on. "Either time. Naturally you thought I'd be on birth control, making advances like that."

"You told me you hadn't had sex since you brought Jimmy home. I had no reason to assume you'd be on birth control."

She shrugged. "True, but that doesn't mean I wasn't on the pill for some medical reason. And I wasn't. I could be pregnant now."

Tara forced herself not to lay a hand over her abdomen. *Chances were slim, right?* "I'm sorry."

"You weren't alone in your actions, you know."

"But you weren't thinking straight. I took advantage of you."

The corner of his mouth lifted. "True. Still, I'd like you to sign these papers."

"Dylan, I can't. I know we've lied about our marriage, but I can't lie anymore."

She turned to leave the room, but he caught her arm.

"Then will you agree to be Lily's guardian?"

Her mouth dropped open. She searched his face as her heart raced. He looked serious. "What?"

"If something happens to me, I want you to raise Lily. She feels safe with you."

"But, Dylan—I mean, of course I'll take care of her, but shouldn't you ask Adam and Anne or your mom or Rosemary's mom?"

"Lily loves you, and I know you'll do right by her."

"This is unbelievable." She laughed, her earlier sadness swept away. *Lily's mom? No, don't get carried away. Just her guardian.* Not much different than what she was doing now. "I'd be glad to, of course. Well, not glad," she amended, "as it would mean something had happened to you."

He grinned. "Gee, thanks."

"I love her. You know I'll take good care of her."

"My lawyer's been bugging me about making a will to provide for Lily, but I couldn't see asking anyone else, and I wasn't sure you'd do it."

"Why wouldn't I? Because I'm not a relative? Or…because our marriage is temporary?"

"What if it wasn't?"

Tara inhaled, spearing him with her gaze. Had she heard correctly? She shook her head, unable to believe her ears.

"Don't say no until you think about it. We work well as a couple. Lily needs a mother," he continued, "and she already loves you. I love Jimmy, and he needs a dad."

"Dylan." She ran her hands into her hair and pulled. "This isn't something you can fix with logic." *I want more. I want your love.*

He frowned. "What are you talking about?"

"I know you. You think everything has a logical answer. That's why you're so good at your job."

He laughed. "You think staying married to you is logical?"

That stung and she couldn't hide her flinch.

"It's not at all logical," he said, "but it's something I want. We have chemistry. The other night proved that." He flashed a grin. "And I'd be happy to prove it again."

Chemistry? He called their lovemaking—the most moving sexual experience of her life—*chemistry?* She could have slapped him. She wanted to tell him it had been only okay, merely passable, barely a blip on her radar.

His smile faded as he took in her expression. "We love each other's child like our own. We get along well." His voice trailed off.

Dylan couldn't say the one thing that would convince her to stay married to him. Because he didn't love her.

"How about we take a belated honeymoon?" he offered.

"I can't talk to you while you're being irrational."

"I'll show you irrational." He pulled her into his arms and kissed her.

She should have struggled. She should have walked away before it got this crazy. She should have…

Not enjoyed it so much.

His hands trailed over her back, pulling her even closer into his body. His kisses stirred her against her will. One more minute, then she'd pull away. Since this would probably be the last time he kissed her, she wanted to remember it. His erection nudged her and she longed to press herself against him.

But he hadn't mentioned love.

She turned her head away, gasping. "Stop."

Dylan released his tight grip, and she stepped back.

"This is crazy," she said.

"We could go to Ireland. Mom's postcard claims it's full of magic and you've brought magic to my life. Maybe we could find some together."

She couldn't understand his riddles. "What magic? Getting Lily to sleep, or to look you in the eye, or to stop talking in whispers? That wasn't magic, Dylan."

"You transformed me from a hollow bachelor into a real dad. I didn't even know what was missing from my life until you made it so much better."

"Lily turned you into a real dad. It was mostly you, earning her trust."

"What about the magic I feel when you're in my arms?"

"Sex," she scoffed.

"What about the magic I feel when you say my name? Or how I feel when I come home at night, knowing you're here?"

She eyed him, afraid to believe.

"When I see you in the morning," he continued. "When you're playing with the kids and I just want to sit and soak it all in."

She shook her head.

"I have an early birthday present for you." He pulled something from his pocket and dropped it onto her palm.

A tiny booklet with a black vinyl cover lay in her hand. With a book of matches. "What is it?"

"It's a symbol. It's supposed to be my little black book of phone numbers." He shrugged. "But I don't write them down. I enter them in my phone. I can show you my phone's address book. Totally empty of other women's contact information."

"Why?"

"I want you to give our marriage a chance. I thought—I hoped—this gesture would tell you something."

"You're giving up other women?"

"I gave them up when you agreed to marry me."

"What if I say no? You've got a backup copy, right?"

Dylan shook his head.

"Wow." Could he be serious? "I don't know what to say."

"Say you'll give me another chance. Say you want to stay married."

"There's so much more at stake here than what I want, Dylan."

"I understand that. You need to do what's right for Jimmy."

She nodded.

He reached into his desk drawer and handed her a large brown envelope.

Mystified, she pulled out more legal papers. All she needed from him was a declaration of love. The words on the paper sharpened her attention. "How did you get Jay to do this?"

Dylan smiled. "Your ex-boyfriend needs gambling money. Jay is proud of his name, but he isn't ready for a child."

Jay had signed away his parental rights, erasing the threat of a future custody battle.

"His family will want to visit, but that'll be a good thing."

"And he's letting me adopt Jimmy."

Her gaze shot to his.

"Well, not me, specifically," Dylan backpedaled. "He signed off for someone you approve of to adopt Jimmy, though. I just hope it's me someday."

"You paid him for Jimmy?" She didn't know if she was more scandalized or thrilled.

"Of course not. No one has that kind of money. The kid's priceless." Dylan shifted. "I just exchanged money for Jamison's signature on the form."

"Where did you get the money? From my parents?"

"I sold the condo."

She stood openmouthed. "But now you don't have any place to go."

A smile wobbled on his lips. "I took a gamble, my-self."

Tara was stunned that he'd leave himself so vulnerable. She couldn't find words to express how deeply his gesture touched her. He'd given up his last refuge of freedom?

"But," he said, "if you don't want me to stay, Lily and I can move into Mom's until we find a place. Her house is empty for another few weeks."

He'd misread her inability to speak as rejection.

"What if I want you to stay?" she asked.

He took her hand and stared into her eyes.

"I love you, Tara." He swallowed hard. "And I think, I hope, you can come to love me. Maybe you already do, a little?"

Again she shook her head, this time to clear her dizzi-ness. Had he actually said he loved her?

"Oh," he said. "So why do you want me to stay?"

"I don't love you a little, Dylan." She grinned.

His face lit with cautious hope. "Tell me."

"I love you with my heart, and my whole life. I want to be beside you while we raise Jimmy and Lily. I hope I am pregnant with your baby."

His eyes widened before he threw back his head and laughed. "I can help with that."

His kiss started tender, then deepened, his hands as busy as hers.

"I hope so," she said. "I don't want to fill the house like Adam and Anne, but a couple more would be nice. A sister and a brother for each."

Somehow they'd ended up lying down on the couch. She was fuzzy on the details. "I've loved you for a while now. I'm surprised you couldn't tell."

"I had no idea. I've loved you almost from the day we met. Why else would I have asked you to marry me?"

"Because of Lily, of course."

He kissed her nose. "Do you really think I couldn't have outlasted her tears?"

"But—"

He kissed her jawline up to her ear, down the curve of her cheek. "Do you really think I couldn't have come up with some other solution?"

Tara couldn't speak for a few minutes, parrying with his tongue in her mouth. She wanted to laugh and scream her joy from the roof.

"You're the love of my life, Tara. How about I have my lawyer draw up adoption papers?"

"Oh, Dylan." Her heart caught. "Yes. Do you think it's too soon?"

"Lily loves you."

"Have Rosemary's mother send us a picture of Rosemary. I'll help Lily put it in her room. She can have two mothers."

"Do you think Jimmy's ready?" Dylan shook his head. "Never mind."

"Jimmy loves you." She smiled, remembering his support of Jimmy when Jay had visited. "And you look alike."

He smiled back. "We have the same middle name."

"There you go then. It's fate."

"I agree. Fate brought us together." He kissed her, drawing the sweetness of the moment into heat. "I have another present for you."

"I don't need anything else but you."

"Then take it as a present *to* me."

She looked at him quizzically. He went back to his desk and returned with a small box. Kneeling beside the couch, he presented her with a sapphire solitaire. "I'd be honored if you'd wear this."

"An engagement ring?"

He nodded.

"But we're already married. I have this." She held out her hand, displaying the silver band he'd given her at the wedding. "This is the one that counts."

"This is a symbol." Dylan slipped the ring from the box and held it by the sides, ready to place it on her finger. "Wearing this is your promise to love me and stay with me forever. I give it to you, promising I'll love you and stay with you forever."

He gazed into her eyes. "I want it all. You, the kids, everything. Will you wear it?"

She nodded, tears in her eyes as he slid it onto her finger, securing it against her wedding ring. "I'll take it all."

"Now there's just one more problem to take care of."

"What's that?" she asked.

Dylan grinned. "I'm getting a little cramped sleeping on the couch."

Tara's heartbeat raced in anticipation. She stood and extended a hand. "Come on, husband. I'll show you where your bed is."

* * * * *

COMING NEXT MONTH

Available June 14, 2011

You can find more information on upcoming
Harlequin® titles, free excerpts and more at
www.HarlequinInsideRomance.com.

REQUEST YOUR FREE BOOKS!
2 FREE NOVELS PLUS 2 FREE GIFTS!

LOVE, HOME & HAPPINESS

YES! Please send me 2 FREE Harlequin American Romance® novels and my 2 FREE gifts (gifts are worth about $10). After receiving them, if I don't wish to receive any more books, I can return the shipping statement marked "cancel." If I don't cancel, I will receive 4 brand-new novels every month and be billed just $4.24 per book in the U.S. or $4.99 per book in Canada. That's a saving of at least 15% off the cover price! It's quite a bargain! Shipping and handling is just 50¢ per book in the U.S. and 75¢ per book in Canada.* I understand that accepting the 2 free books and gifts places me under no obligation to buy anything. I can always return a shipment and cancel at any time. Even if I never buy another book, the two free books and gifts are mine to keep forever.

154/354 HDN FDKS

Name _____ (PLEASE PRINT)

Address _____ Apt. #

City _____ State/Prov. _____ Zip/Postal Code

Signature (if under 18, a parent or guardian must sign)

Mail to the **Reader Service:**
IN U.S.A.: P.O. Box 1867, Buffalo, NY 14240-1867
IN CANADA: P.O. Box 609, Fort Erie, Ontario L2A 5X3

Not valid for current subscribers to Harlequin American Romance books.

Want to try two free books from another line?
Call 1-800-873-8635 or visit www.ReaderService.com.

* Terms and prices subject to change without notice. Prices do not include applicable taxes. Sales tax applicable in N.Y. Canadian residents will be charged applicable taxes. Offer not valid in Quebec. This offer is limited to one order per household. All orders subject to credit approval. Credit or debit balances in a customer's account(s) may be offset by any other outstanding balance owed by or to the customer. Please allow 4 to 6 weeks for delivery. Offer available while quantities last.

Your Privacy—The Reader Service is committed to protecting your privacy. Our Privacy Policy is available online at www.ReaderService.com or upon request from the Reader Service.

We make a portion of our mailing list available to reputable third parties that offer products we believe may interest you. If you prefer that we not exchange your name with third parties, or if you wish to clarify or modify your communication preferences, please visit us at www.ReaderService.com/consumerschoice or write to us at Reader Service Preference Service, P.O. Box 9062, Buffalo, NY 14269. Include your complete name and address.

HARII

Harlequin® Blaze™ brings you
New York Times *and* USA TODAY *bestselling author*
Vicki Lewis Thompson with three new steamy titles
from the bestselling miniseries SONS OF CHANCE

Chance isn't just the last name of these rugged
Wyoming cowboys—it's their motto, too!

Read on for a sneak peek at the first title,
SHOULD'VE BEEN A COWBOY

Available June 2011 only from Harlequin® Blaze™.

"THANKS FOR NOT TURNING ON THE LIGHTS," Tyler said. "I'm a mess."

"Not in my book." Even in low light, Alex had a good view of her yellow shirt plastered to her body. It was all he could do not to reach for her, mud and all. But the next move needed to be hers, not his.

She slicked her wet hair back and squeezed some water out of the ends as she glanced upward. "I like the sound of the rain on a tin roof."

"Me, too."

She met his gaze briefly and looked away. "Where's the sink?"

"At the far end, beyond the last stall."

Tyler's running shoes squished as she walked down the aisle between the rows of stalls. She glanced sideways at Alex. "So how much of a cowboy are you these days? Do you ride the range and stuff?"

"I ride." He liked being able to say that. "Why?"

"Just wondered. Last summer, you were still a city boy. You even told me you weren't the cowboy type, but you're…different now."

HBEXP0611

He wasn't sure if that was a good thing or a bad thing. Maybe she preferred city boys to cowboys. "How am I different?"

"Well, you dress differently, and your hair's a little longer. Your face seems a little more chiseled, but maybe that's because of your hair. Also, there's something else, something harder to define, an attitude…"

"Are you saying I have an attitude?"

"Not in a bad way. It's more like a quiet confidence."

He was flattered, but still he had to laugh. "I just admitted a while ago that I have all kinds of doubts about this event tomorrow. That doesn't seem like quiet confidence to me."

"This isn't about your job, it's about…your…" She took a deep breath. "It's about your sex appeal, okay? I have no business talking about it, because it will only make me want to do things I shouldn't do." She started toward the end of the barn. "Now, where's that sink? We need to get cleaned up and go back to the house. Dinner is probably ready, and I—"

He spun her around and pulled her into his arms, mud and all. "Let's do those things." Then he kissed her, knowing that she would kiss him back, knowing that this time he would take that kiss where he wanted it to go. And she would let him.

Follow Tyler and Alex's wild adventures in
SHOULD'VE BEEN A COWBOY
Available June 2011 only from Harlequin® Blaze™
wherever books are sold.

SPECIAL EDITION

Life, Love and Family

LOVE CAN BE FOUND IN THE MOST UNLIKELY PLACES, ESPECIALLY WHEN YOU'RE NOT LOOKING FOR IT...

Failed marriages, broken families and disappointment. Cecilia and Brandon have both been unlucky in love and life and are ripe for an intervention. Good thing Brandon's mother happens to stumble upon this matchmaking project. But will Brandon be able to open his eyes and get away from his busy career to see that all he needs is right there in front of him?

FIND OUT IN
WHAT THE SINGLE DAD WANTS...

BY *USA TODAY* BESTSELLING AUTHOR
MARIE FERRARELLA

**AVAILABLE IN JUNE 2011
WHEREVER BOOKS ARE SOLD.**